ture & eisure Services

D0295304

NEW YEAR'S RESOLUTIONS!

Resolutions are made to be broken...!

Childhood friends Mira and Ellory each make a New Year's Resolution to *stay away from love*. Little do they know that fate has other things in mind...

When two hunky doctors hit the slopes, escaping their past in the deep snowy mountains, the last thing they expect to find is two wonderful women who can heal minds, bodies and souls...and maybe these brooding doctors' hearts!

This New Year, lose yourself in these magical snowy romances from Mills & Boon® Medical Romance™ authors

Tina Beckett and Amalie Berlin

Read Jack and Mira's story in
HOW TO FIND A MAN IN FIVE DATES

Read Anson and Ellory's story in
BREAKING HER NO-DATING RULE

Dear Reader

I seem to have a love/hate relationship with New Year's resolutions. I love making them. Keeping them? Hmm…not so much.

When the heroine of HOW TO FIND A MAN IN FIVE DATES makes a crazy resolution one snowy New Year's Eve she has every intention of keeping it. After all, she's fresh out of a disastrous relationship and not looking to start anything new. What she *doesn't* count on, however, is coming to the rescue of a surfer-dude-turned-newbie-skier when he wipes out on his first run down the slopes. What starts off as one date turns into two, and soon she is doing some slipping and sliding of her own…emotionally.

Thank you for joining Mira and Jack as they make their way down a treacherous slope where trust and self-forgiveness become rules to live by—and hopefully find love along the way. I hope you enjoy reading their story as much as I loved writing it!

Have fun on those ski slopes of life—and maybe even break a resolution or two of your own!

Love

Tina Beckett

HOW TO
FIND A MAN
IN FIVE DATES

BY
TINA BECKETT

All rights reserved including the right of reproduction in whole or in part in any form. This edition is published by arrangement with Harlequin Books S.A.

This is a work of fiction. Names, characters, places, locations and incidents are purely fictional and bear no relationship to any real life individuals, living or dead, or to any actual places, business establishments, locations, events or incidents. Any resemblance is entirely coincidental.

This book is sold subject to the condition that it shall not, by way of trade or otherwise, be lent, resold, hired out or otherwise circulated without the prior consent of the publisher in any form of binding or cover other than that in which it is published and without a similar condition including this condition being imposed on the subsequent purchaser.

® and TM are trademarks owned and used by the trademark owner and/or its licensee. Trademarks marked with ® are registered with the United Kingdom Patent Office and/or the Office for Harmonisation in the Internal Market and in other countries.

First published in Great Britain 2015
by Mills & Boon, an imprint of Harlequin (UK) Limited,
Large Print edition 2015
Eton House, 18-24 Paradise Road,
Richmond, Surrey, TW9 1SR

© 2015 Tina Beckett

ISBN: 978-0-263-25486-0

Harlequin (UK) Limited's policy is to use papers that are natural, renewable and recyclable products and made from wood grown in sustainable forests. The logging and manufacturing processes conform to the legal environmental regulations of the country of origin.

Printed and bound in Great Britain
by CPI Antony Rowe, Chippenham, Wiltshire

Born to a family that was always on the move, **Tina Beckett** learned to pack a suitcase almost before she knew how to tie her shoes. Fortunately she met a man who also loved to travel, and she snapped him right up. Married for over twenty years, Tina has three wonderful children and has lived in gorgeous places such as Portugal and Brazil.

Living where English reading material is difficult to find has its drawbacks, however. Tina had to come up with creative ways to satisfy her love for romance novels, so she picked up her pen and tried writing one. After her tenth book she realised she was hooked. She was officially a writer.

A three-time Golden Heart finalist, and fluent in Portuguese, Tina now divides her time between the United States and Brazil. She loves to use exotic locales as the backdrop for many of her stories. When she's not writing you can find her either on horseback or soldering stained glass panels for her home.

Tina loves to hear from readers. You can contact her through her website or 'friend' her on Facebook.

Recent titles by Tina Beckett:

HIS GIRL FROM NOWHERE
TO PLAY WITH FIRE
THE DANGERS OF DATING DR CARVALHO
HER HARD TO RESIST HUSBAND
DOCTOR'S GUIDE TO DATING IN THE JUNGLE
THE LONE WOLF'S CRAVING
NYC ANGELS: FLIRTING WITH DANGER

These books are also available in eBook format from www.millsandboon.co.uk

**Praise for
Tina Beckett:**

'…a tension-filled emotional story with just
the right amount of drama. The author's vivid
description of the Brazilian jungle and its
people make this story something special.'
—*RT Book Reviews* on
DOCTOR'S GUIDE
TO DATING IN THE JUNGLE

'Medical Romance™ lovers will definitely like
NYC ANGELS: FLIRTING WITH DANGER
by Tina Beckett—for who *doesn't* like
a good forbidden romance?'
—*HarlequinJunkie* on
NYC ANGELS: FLIRTING WITH DANGER

PROLOGUE

HERE'S TO A brand-new year.

Dr. Miranda Dupris clutched her empty champagne flute and waited for the dreaded annual countdown to begin. The huge gathering area of her father's lodge—with its vaulted ceilings and blazing fireplace—was packed, the free food and drinks drawing in legions of guests and employees, all hoping the year ahead would be kinder than the one they were leaving behind.

Or maybe that was just her.

A fresh glass of glittery amber liquid was pressed into her hand, while the empty one was plucked free and deposited onto the tray of one of the serving staff. The smell of champagne clogged her senses, its sharp bite a welcome diversion.

"Mira, we totally forgot to make our resolutions!" Her best friend grinned at her, long blonde curls bouncing as she swirled the contents of her own glass. "Let's do them now. That way you can dump Robert into the universe's nearest black hole and start over."

At the mention of her ex-fiancé, Mira curled her toes into the ankle-slaying red stilettos while the familiar sting of betrayal lanced through her gut.

Never again. Never, *ever* again.

If anyone was jumping into the nearest black hole, it was going to be her.

She was done with relationships. For good this time. Three failed engagements in the last seven years should tell her something.

"I'm all for that." She forced her lips to tilt upward, trying not to ruin their New Year's Eve tradition, something she and Ellory had done for the last ten years in this very room. She lifted her glass. "I'll even go first. I hereby swear off committed relationships for the next twelve months."

Her friend laughed. "What about uncommitted ones?"

What about them?

Oh! Her foggy brain finally put two and two

together. Ellory was asking if she was swearing off men altogether. Was she?

Maybe that was a bit too extreme. She did *like* men. Some of them, anyway. Just not certain bastardly ski instructors.

"Uncommitted is good. More than good, actually." She raised her glass even higher. "Okay, how about this, then? I resolve to date twenty-five men over the next year with no emotional involvement whatsoever. Zip. *Nada.*"

Her friend blinked. "Whoa." Ellory now had to yell over the crowd as the clock hands on the huge screen across from them shifted closer and closer to the witching hour. "Are you serious? Miss Monogamy Dupris is going to serial date?"

Um…yes. Why not?

The idea sounded more and more attractive. Or maybe that was the three glasses of champagne she'd had. Whatever. She took another bracing sip. "That's exactly what I'm going to do. Serial date. Twenty-five men…one year."

"This I've got to see. Bet you a hundred bucks you either back out or you don't make it past man number five without getting attached to him."

Ha! Unless the fifth guy was a puppy hiding in a man suit, she didn't see that happening.

"Make it *ten* men. No, wait…all twenty-five. And backing out is not an option." She waggled her shoulders back and forth, her courage growing with each passing moment. "Tell you what. Next New Year's Eve we'll see who pays whom. Your turn. What's your resolution? And it'd better be good!"

"Well, if you can swear off serious relationships, I can swear off men altogether—maybe work on myself for a change, take on a project. And I'll bet the same amount of money that I *will* follow through." Ellory's expression had taken on a serious note, totally out of character for her fun-loving friend.

But with the hands almost at the top of the dial, she didn't have time to question her. "Okay, so we each have a hundred dollars riding on our resolutions, right?"

"Right."

She'd just gotten the words out when a cacophony of voices began chanting backwards from ten. Ellory clinked her glass against Mira's and they downed the last of their drinks.

Confetti rained all around her, the cheers and laughter of the crowd forming a frothy wave of mirth that carried her up and out of her funk. Mira caught her friend up in a tight hug, so glad Ellory had come to stay with her for a while.

She stepped back, about to say something, when a masculine voice came from behind her. "Well, well, well. Looks like I'm not the only one without a date tonight. Or are you two together?"

Mira's eyes widened when she realized the slightly slurred tones were far too close to her ear for comfort. Still holding onto one of Ellory's hands, she raised her brows in question. Surely not.

"Turn around," her friend mouthed. "He's talking to you."

Knees quivering, Mira released her hand and pivoted on the spiked heel of her shoe until she was face to face with a beefy hunk who could have stepped straight out of an ad for a gym membership. He was tall and buff, and his too-tanned-to-be-real neck rose from a pressed white shirt and black tux. His blue eyes gleamed with something that looked like…interest. Or boredom. She couldn't decide which.

"I—I…" Her mind went blank, and she scrabbled for the nearest coherent sentence. "Er… hello."

How the hell did one serial date, anyway? She'd have to ask Ellory for some pointers later.

The man's smile grew. "I waited a whole ten minutes to make sure no irate boyfriend was going to bust my jaw for coming over here. I noticed you as soon as you walked through the door. Are you alone?"

Oh, no. Not this fast.

She glanced back at her friend, who opened her beaded purse and tipped it toward her with a knowing jiggle. "You want to pay up now, honey?"

Egads. The woman knew right where to hit.

Straightening her spine, she turned back to the man in question. "Yep. I'm alone."

"What say I buy you a drink, then?"

Since the booze was free, that was hardly an

enticing offer. But if her job was to stay unattached, this guy seemed like the obvious choice.

"What say you do?" Mira tried for a purr, but it came off sounding like an asthmatic wheeze.

Before she could chicken out, she handed her empty champagne glass to Ellory, who stared at her with undisguised shock. Mira leaned forward and whispered two words, drawing them out for emphasis. "Game. On."

CHAPTER ONE

JACKSON PERRY WAS going to fall.

No matter how many times he tried to stab his ski poles into the snow, they ended up flailing around like twin javelins about to be launched by a drunken athlete.

Make your skis into a wedge to slow your rate of descent.

The instructor's mandatory lesson played through his skull, but actually obeying that advice was almost impossible, since he was too busy trying to find his center of gravity as his body continued to pick up speed down the slope. He tried to ride it out like a surfer on a killer wave. Only skis were nothing like the smooth, wide surface of his well-waxed board. And the ground looked a whole lot harder than the soft embrace of the ocean.

Wobble.

Correct.

Wobble.

Correct.

Not. Gonna. Freakin'. Work…

A brilliant plume of white spray rose up as Jack belly-flopped onto the snow, his skis detaching from his boots—*thank God.* He bounced his way over some moguls, instinctively tightening his abs to absorb as much of the impact as possible. Fifty yards later he slid to an ignominious halt, still facing the bottom of the hill. He had one pole in his hand, the other was long gone, probably back there with his skis.

Good thing he hadn't tried a tougher slope.

Sucking down breaths into lungs that felt like they were on fire, he assessed his body bone by bone, tendon by tendon. Knees? Undamaged. Wrists? Still there. Ego? He'd come back to that one later. Skull? Intact, although he wondered about his sanity in agreeing to this damned vacation.

He raised a hand to wipe away some of the snow on his face, only to find his gloves were also covered in the stuff.

Hell!

Take a vacation. Have some fun. You need a break.

Or else.

His coach may not have added those last two words, but Jack had seen them written in the tight lines of the man's face when he'd been late to yet another early morning meeting. The product of a recurring nightmare followed up by a sleeping pill. He hadn't even heard the alarm the next morning.

Go skiing, Jack...or I'm afraid we'll have to find ourselves a new doctor.

So, was the plan working?

Oh, yeah. So far, he was having a blast.

And every damn memory he'd been trying to forget had followed him right down that hill, crashing into the snow beside him.

Several more skiers sailed by, none of them seeming to have any trouble with the so-called "bunny slope." Nothing like wiping out on your very first run.

A pair of skis came into view. Angled just like the instructor had described. *Perfect.* He glanced up, squinting to see past the blinding midmorning sun.

"Need some help there?"

A vision in a white ski jacket and matching snow pants stood before him, the light seeming to halo around the figure's shoulders and head.

Maybe he'd hit the ground harder than he'd thought.

He shook his head and then struggled into a sitting position, but the slick fabric of his own suit caused him to slide down the hill a few more feet. The person matched his downward trajectory inch for inch, again coming to a halt right as he did. Still on her feet.

A quick feminine laugh met his ears. "Here, take my hand. Your boots should help you gain some traction. I've already picked up your skis and pole."

He glanced up again and saw that the woman—and she was definitely a woman—did indeed have his errant equipment caged in the crook of her arm. A white-gloved hand stretched down toward him.

Definitely not a beginner. At least, he hoped

not, otherwise he might as well throw in the towel and stick to football and watersports.

"I'm good." The last thing he wanted was to bring her down with him. He struggled to his feet, somehow succeeding on the first try. She was right, though, about the boots giving him traction.

"Think you can make it to the bottom?" She flipped her goggles up over her head, causing the fur-trimmed hood of her jacket to fall back, revealing a pink knit aviator hat. Soft brown eyes that were alight with humor regarded him.

She'd probably get a lot of mileage out of this story over drinks with her friends later on.

She was exactly what he pictured when he thought of snow bunnies, from her matchy-matchy suit to her obvious ease in the frigid environment. Even her complexion was pale and frosty, with just a touch of pink warming her lips and cheeks. Cool and untouchable. All except for the flaming locks now visible from beneath her hat.

Just like Paula's hair had been. His teeth clenched.

"Are you okay?" she asked.

Right. She was still waiting for him to tell her if he could make it down the hill.

"I'll be fine from here. Thanks again for the help. If you'll just hand me my gear…"

"First time on the slopes?"

Wasn't it obvious? A spark of male pride urged him to tell her that he'd once competed in some of the biggest surfing competitions California had to offer. But that had been before he'd gotten his medical license and changed his focus to football. Before the accident that had changed his life forever.

Coach was right. He'd let himself go over the last four years.

"Yep." His eyes tracked a little girl zipping down the course with ease. "They make it look so easy."

The woman glanced over her shoulder with a smile. "Yes, they do." She turned back and held out her hand again. "Miranda Dupris."

"Jack Perry." He took her hand and gave it a quick squeeze, suddenly glad they both had on gloves. Even so, something in his gut twisted at the brief contact.

A voice came from the side. "Hey, Florence Nightingale, do you mind clearing the slope? I don't want a pile-up on my watch." His instructor from a few minutes ago pushed his poles into the snow and surged past them, heading on down the hill. He didn't glance their way, but something about the wry twist to his voice said he knew Miranda. Quite well, in fact.

Of course the guy knew her. She was a snow bunny. She probably knew all the instructors by name.

Then a strange thing happened. Instead of waving to the man with a laugh, her brown eyes went from smiling and carefree to cool and irritated in the space of a few seconds.

A woman scorned? Or something else?

"Come on," she said. "I'll buy you a hot chocolate once we get to the bottom."

He almost groaned. He'd been hoping to clomp his way down the hill and head straight to his room, where he could lick his wounded ego in private. The last thing he wanted to do was hang around the bar with a woman who'd seen him at his worst.

He swallowed and retracted that last thought. She hadn't seen him at his worst, but his coach had. Including the twenty pounds he'd shed over the past six months as the dreams had swallowed more and more of his nights and haunted his days. It's what had made the man book this vacation in a frozen wasteland. Why couldn't he have chosen Hawaii instead?

Maybe he could refuse her offer with grace. "No need, but thanks." He held out his hands for the equipment she still held.

"Maybe not, but standing here without working my muscles has made me realize I'm freezing my tushie off, and I could sure use something to warm it back up."

Those words finally yanked him free of his morose thoughts and put them right on...

No, you don't, Perry. Don't you dare look.

Too late. His eyes had already skated over her hips and mentally guessed what lay beneath all those layers of clothing. And it was good.

Wow. If she knew what you were thinking, she'd

dump your gear in the snow and march her oh-so-cold tushie right back down the hill.

Damn. Time to renew his gentleman card. Paula would have given him a single raised eyebrow if she could hear him now.

But she couldn't. Thanks to him. And the coach. And the team.

No. That was no one's fault but his.

Suddenly the last thing he wanted was to be alone. Even if it meant spending a half-hour with a woman who'd probably made the rounds more than he had during his entire internship. "Hot chocolate sounds good. Thanks."

She gave him a quick grin and handed him his equipment. "Don't hurry, unless you enjoy sliding down the hill. I'll meet you at the bottom."

With that, she turned around and pushed off, her skis flashing as she leaned forward and took the slope like an expert.

Sighing, Jack juggled his poles and his skis and took his first shaky step.

Did forcing someone to drink hot chocolate count as date number five? Mira scrunched her nose as she waited for her next victim to finish trudging his way down the hill. She wouldn't have pushed so hard if it hadn't been for that Florence Nightingale crack Robert had made as he'd sailed past her.

Yes, it was spiteful to head for the bar with another man when she knew her ex was there on his break, but she wanted to make it as plain as the icicles hanging from the man's heart that she was done. No amount of sweet-talking would get her to take him back. Seducing your female students was not part of a ski instructor's job description, no matter what most people thought.

Ellory was right. She needed to move on. Not getting emotionally attached was something that came hard for her, but if she kept choosing men who were not her type, it should be a breeze.

Jack Perry was definitely on the "not" side of the equation. Her newly written "not" side, anyway.

With his chiseled, clean-shaven jaw and refusal to let her help him up, he was evidently a man's man, something she was now avoiding like the plague as far as relationships went. She'd been there, done that—three times, in fact—and had the heartbreak to prove it. The next guy she got serious with was going to be a poet. Or an artist. Someone who was in touch with his feminine side.

There was nothing feminine about the man she'd met on the slopes. She'd bet he was an athlete—from the easy way his wiry muscles had pushed him up off the ground. Yeah, he might have crashed and burned on that slope, but that was from lack of experience, not lack of strength. Those glutes had some power behind them.

Something she was better off not thinking about.

Hot chocolate. Nothing else. She might have joked with Ellory about bedding a man or two during the next year, but she wasn't planning on actually doing that. Too dangerous. For her, anyway. The words sex and casual? An oxymoron. It always became personal.

So far she'd racked up three losers. Three men who couldn't resist the thrill of the chase, even when that chase involved someone other than their fiancée.

No more bad boys for her.

Surely after a year of empty dates she'd be able to tell the difference between a player and a guy who was capable of monogamy. Until then, she had to stick to the plan.

But, man, oh, man, as Jack sidled the last twenty feet, making short work of each step in those heavy boots, he was making her little heart go pitter-patter.

Reaching down to undo her skis when she realized she'd been watching him instead of attending to her own business, she stepped out of them and hefted them upright. "Ready?" she asked, when he reached her.

"Yes." His voice was a little tighter than it had been up the hill, although she didn't see how that could be, since he hadn't been jumping for joy at the thought of spending some time with her. She'd had the opposite problem with man number three. He hadn't exactly been happy when she'd closed the door to her room with him on the wrong side of it.

Well, from Jack's guarded expression, getting rid of him should be a snap.

They turned in their skis and poles at the equipment center next to the ski lodge and then Mira led the way into the foyer of the main building. The familiar honeyed tones of wood-covered floors and walls welcomed her like a snug, warm cocoon, especially when compared to the vast snow-covered surfaces outside its doors. The crackle of the fire in the huge stone fireplace in the middle of the room only added to that sense of welcome.

Moving over to the long hallway lined with pegs and cubbies, she shimmied out of her jacket and hung it up along with her hat. As she ran her fingers through her hair to fluff it up a bit, she was far too aware of the man next to her shuffling out of his own coat and snow pants. She smiled at the snug black jeans he had on beneath his clothes. And, man, she was so right about those glutes.

Damn!

He swung back around, catching her in the act. One brow lifted, and his lips tightened just a touch. So he didn't like her looking. Well, it wasn't as if he hadn't checked her out on the slope. She'd seen those dark eyes skim over her in quick appraisal. Right after her ex had zoomed past, like the jerk he was.

Forget about Robert. He was not on her current shopping list. Jack was.

She refreshed her memory about the goals of this particular encounter: have a quick cup of cocoa and then she was free to move on.

To man number six.

CHAPTER TWO

JACK'S SKI INSTRUCTOR was currently staring at his rescuer. And not a subtle kind of stare, either. This was a full-on, you-*will*-look-at-me kind of unwavering attention.

And yet as Miranda set their drinks down, she was chatting away as if she had no idea.

He gave himself a mental palm to the head. Of course. She had to be a ski instructor as well. No wonder she'd helped him up and made sure he got down the hill. It also explained why the other guy had told her to clear him off the slope.

What it didn't explain was why the man was now staring at them.

Best to settle this right here and now, in case this was a pity drink. Surely he didn't look that badly off. He'd have to work on his cheerful see-ya-later grin. "You don't have to sit with me. I'm fine, really."

She frowned. "Never thought you weren't. I'm sitting here because I'm cold and tired and wanted some hot chocolate."

"I didn't see you up at the top when I was having my lesson."

"That's because I wasn't there. I was skiing one of the harder slopes. I decided to finish up on the bunny. As a cool down."

Cool down. No wonder she was in such great shape. And she was. He might deny it until he was blue in the face, but he'd glanced at her a time or two. Enough to know that her slender legs were strong. So were her arms. If he'd met her anywhere else, he might think she was a distance runner. But she wasn't. She was a skier.

"I bet you have to rescue lots of guys like me." The second the words were out of his mouth he wished he could retract them. He hadn't needed rescuing. Not on the slopes, and certainly not anywhere else, despite what his coach might think.

He could have handled things himself, given a little more time.

Yeah? Like he'd handled those dreams? Popping sleeping pills like they were candy was not the best prescription—as he'd soon discovered. The good thing was he'd almost weaned himself from them. The nightmares were back, but maybe they were just something he'd have to live with. Like his guilt.

"Not too many rescues. Just the occasional stray."

She picked up her chocolate and took a long sip. "Ah. Just what I needed. Something to keep me warm and happy." Before he could dwell too long on those words, she continued. "So where are you from?"

Four years ago that would have been an easy question to answer. He would have asked whether she meant originally or at the moment. As it was, he wasn't sure of his actual location. Halfway between anger and grief, if he had to guess, a place he'd been stuck at for far too long. "California, originally, but I live in Texas now. And you?"

"Silver Pass. Born and raised right here on the mountain." She raised her mug and took another drink.

So why didn't she seem thrilled to live in a gorgeous place like this? He took a gulp of his own hot chocolate and then sputtered when an unexpected burn slid down his throat.

"Hot?" She gave him a grin that could only be described as mischievous.

"No. Spiked." His brows drew together. "How do you know I'm not an alcoholic?"

"Are you?"

He could have been, but a couple of years ago he'd realized drinking was not only *not* helping him but it could get someone hurt. His team relied on him to make good decisions. One wrong move and a career could be finished forever. Much like his had almost been.

It's why he'd agreed with the coach about this vacation spot. The cold climate kind of fostered isolation. At least in his head it did. With all that gear on, it wasn't very easy to talk to strangers. It wasn't the same as lying on a beach or surfing. Because the waves always carried you back in to shore. With skiing, you could simply race away from strangers who were a little too anxious to start a conversation.

Like this one?

"No, I'm not an alcoholic," he admitted, although the steamy brew slid down his throat in a way that was a little too comforting. He took one more long pull and then set it aside. He wasn't going to switch one habit for another.

Miranda studied him for a few seconds. She started to say something then the instructor who'd been watching her from across the room appeared beside the table. "You headed back for the slopes, Mira? If so, I'll ride up the lift with you."

The guy pointedly ignored Jack, which was fine. He had no intention of stepping in between these two.

"I think I'll go back to my room and read instead. And I can catch up on some reports, while I'm there." The chill in her voice was unmistakable.

"Mira—"

She held up her hand. "I'd rather not do this right now."

The man's lips thinned. "You can't avoid me forever, you know. We both live here. Eventually, we're going to have to sit down and talk."

Jack's glance went to where her left hand gripped her mug. No ring. But there was a definite indentation there.

That's why he'd been staring at her. These two had been involved at some point. Married? An affair, maybe?

Whatever it was, it was none of his business. In fact, maybe it was time for him to take his pity party somewhere else and let these two go at it in private.

Mira beat him to it, standing up, her chin angled at a dangerous height. "I don't see what we have to talk about."

"How happy do you think your father is going to be once he hears about all this?"

She gave a hard smile. "You're right, Robert. I imagine he won't be very happy at all."

Jack was surprised to see the other man's face drain of color.

So that's how it was. The jerk had done something. Something bad enough to make her want to avoid any contact with him. A dark thought came over him.

When the guy reached out to take hold of her

arm Jack rose to his feet, no longer trying to remain impassive. He held the man's gaze for ten
long seconds before "Robert" backed down.

"I'll catch you later," he said to Mira.

"Don't think so. Let's just stick to our own
sides of the slopes."

With an irritated roll of his shoulders the man
spun away from them and stalked toward the
nearest exit.

Mira dropped back into her seat. "Well, it looks
like we're even. I rescued you. You rescued me.
Thanks." She sighed. "Sorry you had to witness
that, though."

"No problem. Ex…" He had no idea why he
gave that leading sentence.

"Fiancé. But that's neither here nor there." She
pursed her lips. "You shouldn't go up on that
slope again without another lesson or two. Next
time you could really get hurt."

If she was worried about her ex pulling something, she needn't bother. He could take care of
himself. "I'll do that."

She must have sensed he was just handing her
a line. "No, I'm serious. Robert's not going to

be a happy camper, so I wouldn't count on him playing nice." She eyed him. "I could give you some pointers if you want. Make sure you stay out of trouble."

That was pretty much impossible. He'd stayed in trouble in one form or another for the last four years. Maybe he should have asked for the beach-front condo vacation despite his earlier thoughts. At least surfing was something he was actually proficient at.

"I don't want to put you to any trouble. I think I can manage."

"Like you did today? Come on. I really do want to show my appreciation."

It was either accept graciously or be a jerk about it. "Did I look that bad out there?"

She laughed. "You want honesty or a gentle lie?"

He found himself smiling back. "Hmm...I'd take the lie, but I think it's already too late for that. Okay, I'll accept the pointers, but I don't guarantee I'll show much improvement. I'm a beachside kind of guy."

"So you're better on the surf than on the turf?"

His smile grew. "No, the turf I can handle. It's cold, slippery surfaces that I struggle with."

"Interesting. So, are we on?"

Why did that seem like a loaded question all of a sudden? But unless he wanted to make a big deal out of what was probably an innocent offer, it was better to let it slide on by. "Yep."

"Great!" She paused to wave at someone across the room. A blonde grinned and held up five fingers.

Mira nodded.

They must be meeting up in a few minutes or something. That was his cue to leave. "What time were you thinking tomorrow?"

"Does tennish work for you?"

"Sounds perfect." He stood. "Thanks for the hot chocolate."

"No problem. I'll see you tomorrow." With one last smile she picked up her cup and headed over to where the other woman was standing. And heaven help him if he didn't watch her hips bump and sway for a couple of beats before forcing himself to turn away.

It's not a date. She hadn't even used that word.

Why he needed to explain that to himself he had no idea. All he knew was that his heart rate had just kicked up a notch and a zing of anticipation was edging through his veins, picking up momentum as it went.

This could be bad.

Very, very bad.

Unless he nipped it in the bud right here. Right now.

The only question…was how.

"Where did you get your goggles?"

Mira peered into her patient's red, streaming eyes as he sat on the exam table in her tiny clinic. Around twenty-two years old, he was here for a week with several buddies. Yesterday evening, after coming off the slopes, his eyes had begun burning. When he'd looked into the mirror that morning, he'd been shocked to see his lids were swollen and his eyes looked terrible.

"I picked up all my gear at a second-hand store right before coming. It was a bargain."

And like any other bargain, sometimes you

paid the price later on. Mira had found that out the hard way when it came to relationships.

She clicked off her penlight and leaned back to check out the eyewear lying beside him. They had the customary reflective surface, but there were no markings that indicated the UV protection the lenses offered. "Your goggles and skis are two pieces of equipment you really shouldn't skimp on. This is why."

"What do you mean?"

"Ever hear of snow blindness?"

Her patient scrubbed moisture from his cheeks. "Snow blindness. Doesn't that only happen to people who are stranded in the snow?"

"Nope. I see it fairly often up here. It's basically a sunburn of your corneas."

He blinked, squinting one eye to look at her. "Can you treat it?"

Swiveling around to her desk, she pulled her prescription pad forward and started writing. "I'm going to give you a prescription for some eyedrops, but you need to stay off the slopes for the next couple of days. Believe me, your eyes aren't going to want to face any light, much less what you'll find up there on the mountain."

"But we're only here for a week."

She felt for him, really she did. "I know. I wish there were a quick treatment, but it's just like any other sunburn. You have to stay out of the sun for a while." She glanced up. "Oh, and make sure you see an eye doctor when you get home."

The man swore a couple of times before finally nodding and taking the slip of paper. He then took his goggles and dumped them in the trash. "I guess I won't be needing those any more."

She smiled. "We have some regulation eyewear at the rental kiosk. Make sure your friends are covered, so they don't wind up in the same boat."

"I will. Thanks, Doc."

"You're welcome."

Once he left, she locked up the clinic and headed up the mountain to meet Jack. It was still a little early, but she wanted to make sure she arrived before he did so she could prepare herself.

Man number five.

Okay, so the guy was cuter than the other men she'd met for drinks or a quick trip down the slopes. In fact, she'd been with one such guy yesterday on the advanced slopes. She had finished on the bunny slope in order to cool down—like she'd told Jack—but only because guy number four had seemed to have hands that never stopped finding excuses to touch her in little ways. Add him to the guy she'd been with two nights ago, and she began to wonder about the wisdom of her resolution. How did serial daters go about avoiding the creeps…and worse?

She needed to be a little more careful about picking these guys. She certainly didn't want to get in over her head. Ellory had forced her to put her cellphone number on speed dial, so Mira could reach out with the touch of a button in case she got into trouble.

She didn't plan on that happening. So far it had just been the two weirdos. Of course, since she'd only been out with four guys in all over the last several weeks, that wasn't much of a track record.

And what about Jack? She'd never been out with a surfer dude before. Although the serious guy who'd sat across from her at the table yesterday did not match her image of a California beach bum.

Just look at the way he'd stood up to Robert.

Yeah, that had been a little heady. She hoped seeing her with Jack had drilled it into her ex's brain that she was moving on—whether it was true or not. Robert had blown it. She'd learned the hard way not to give people second chances.

That included him, and it included her father.

This might be her dad's resort, and he technically might be her boss, but that didn't mean she was going to fall all over him. He'd hurt her mother badly. And even though her mom had been the one to convince her to come back to the lodge and work after she graduated from medical school, she didn't forgive him for his transgressions any more than she'd forgive Robert or her two other exes.

It was exactly why she'd sworn off men. And if she could just get past man number five and move on to the next guy, she'd officially win her bet with Ellory.

Should be a snap.

She leaned on the rail and surveyed the line of chairs on the ski lift.

Speaking of bets, she spied Jack about halfway up the mountain. His safety bar had not been pulled down, making her frown. She'd have to add that to the lesson.

She sucked down a deep breath as he drew closer. She'd just about convinced herself that he wasn't as good looking as she'd thought he was yesterday. But he was. Even from this distance. With streaky brown hair that was in need of a cut and those broad shoulders, he pretty much filled the chair. She'd have to tuck herself under his arm to fit on there with him if they ever rode up together.

The image made her swallow. Silly. *You're here to teach him to ski and put a notch in your...* Hmm, what should she notch, since she had no intentions of sleeping with him or any other of her dates?

Her skis, that's what. Okay, so he'd be one more notch in her skis.

He slid off the chair with lithe grace that had been lacking yesterday when he'd smacked the ground and slid to a halt. How that must have cost him in the ego department. Except he just stood there.

"Slide over here."

He glanced over and saw her then eased down the hill to meet her, a little less shaky than he'd been yesterday.

She had a feeling he'd be a quick study when it came to skiing. Well, whether he was or wasn't, it didn't matter. This would be his one and only lesson with her—a favor for saving her from Robert's pestering. Tomorrow he'd be on his own.

"Hi." He pulled a hat down over his head, juggling his poles as he did so.

At least he'd remembered to put his skis on before getting on the lift. She checked out his eyewear, nodding at the item in his hand. "Did you get those here at the resort?"

He glanced down at them. "Yes, why?"

"Just wondering. Don't want you to get snow blindness."

His brows went up, but he didn't question her comment.

"You ready?" she asked.

"I have to admit I thought about standing you up."

Interesting. He had seemed a little skittish at the bar yesterday.

"Yeah? Well, I'd have had to come and track you down." Ellory had spied Jack from across the room yesterday after her encounter with Robert and claimed that this time she was going down hard. This one was just too yummy for her to resist.

Oh, she could resist him all right. He was just one more guy. In fact, it was quite liberating to be with a man and know there was no future in it. She didn't have to worry about whether or not she'd have to watch her words or get all prettied up.

The time she'd spent in front of the mirror this morning had been strictly about personal grooming. She'd do that for anyone. No need to send people scurrying for the nearest exit with her morning rat's nest and dark under-eye circles. And her lips were chapped from the cold, so of course she'd had to put on something to soothe and protect them. The fact that it had a little dab of shine was just a coincidence.

He smiled. "I guess it's a good thing I showed up, then."

"Absolutely." Luckily, Robert was off this morning, so one of the other instructors was working with a small group of newbies. She could have sent Jack to the class, since her professed reason for meeting him was because her ex might do or say something she would end up feeling badly about. But since she'd told Ellory he was man number five…

Really, who would know she didn't meet him?

Ellory, for one.

Yeah, and why was that? Because she couldn't tell a lie worth a damn.

"So, let's start with your skis. You got them on, but it'll help if you know how to click in and out of them quickly."

She gave him a quick lesson on doing just that. Once they were back on, she had him face the bottom of the hill, but with the fronts of his skis pointed toward each other.

"I'm sure Robert showed you, but once you

start out, you're going to want to stay like this. Think of it like a wedge of pizza, only made with skis instead of food. If you keep your skis completely parallel to each other, you'll pick up too much speed, as you found out yesterday. So wedge them just a bit until you get the feel of your angle and speed." She pulled her goggles down over her eyes. "Let's do a practice run. I'll go first and you follow me down, trying to imitate my movements."

He muttered something that she couldn't quite catch before she used her poles to push off. A hard swish behind her said that he'd done the same thing. She concentrated on going as slowly as possible, not an easy task when you were used to zipping down difficult slopes at top speed. Her father had had big plans for her after she'd won several competitions, plans she'd thwarted when she'd decided to become a doctor. What father in his right mind was disappointed when his child decided to become something other than a professional athlete?

Hers.

Then again, he'd disappointed her as well.

She'd changed courses right after her parents had divorced, and, yes, maybe it had been partly to get back at him. But she loved being a doctor, even more than she loved the slopes and the snow. Jack had talked about surfing. The ocean didn't appeal to her at all. She was a mountain girl through and through. She didn't think she even owned a bikini other than the underwear kind.

Jack came up beside her, showing a pretty good sense of balance. And every time she changed the angle of her wedge, he imitated her. Out of nowhere came the thought that it might be worth a trip to the ocean just to see him up on a surfboard, that streaky hair of his catching rays of sunlight.

He hit a mogul and wavered for a second or two, the tips of his skis wiggling back and forth, but he caught himself. His speed increased fractionally and Mira let off her brake and matched him. "Good job!"

His face was a mask of concentration, so she wasn't even sure whether he'd heard her or not. At that moment someone passed them on the left at a much quicker pace—which wasn't all that difficult, considering she and Jack were creeping along.

Two more people went by.

Mira was concentrating so much on the man beside her that she almost missed the screams from the pair of teens who'd just passed them. They'd gotten too close, and the left ski of the girl closest to them had overlapped the other girl's. Both were struggling to remain upright.

"Move away from each other!" Her training kicked in, knowing if they didn't get their skis apart one or both of them would fall.

They either didn't hear her or were too panicked to do what she said, because they were still tangled. Then one of the girls shoved the other one, maybe to try to push off her and get away. Instead of working, the girl who'd been shoved careened sideways, taking her friend with her. They fell down hard, landing in a heap in the middle of the slope. The girl who'd pushed the other one sat up laughing, but her giggles soon faded when she saw the other teenager lay still in the snow.

Every muscle in Mira's body went on high alert as she drew closer and saw the girl's right arm sticking out at an odd angle.

The uninjured teen must have seen it as well, because she suddenly leaned back and gave out an unearthly shriek.

CHAPTER THREE

"You go down the hill," Mira said. "I need to stay here."

"I can help."

"Just do as I say." Her tone was a little more impatient this time.

He didn't care. "No can do. I'm a doctor."

Mira gave him a sharp look. "Yeah, well, so am I. I'm the concierge doctor for the lodge."

His heart stalled for a second, and he stared, fumbling a bit as he tried to remain upright. "I thought you were a ski instructor."

"Pizza it, Jack, if you want to stop."

He forced his mind back to what she was saying, using his skis to form a barricade and coming to a halt beside the still-screaming girl.

"What's your specialty?" She nudged him aside so she could get to their patients, sinking to her knees in the snow to look at the unconscious teen.

She laid a hand on the panicked girl's shoulder, and like magic she quieted.

He was still struggling to process the fact that he was up on the slopes with a doctor, of all things. "I'm in sports medicine."

Mira's eyes widened when he mentioned the name of the team.

"The Hawks? Are you kidding me?" She gave him another quick glance. "What are you doing skiing, then? Isn't this your busiest time of year?"

No way was he going to tell her he'd been sent off to recuperate. Especially not knowing what he did now. "I'm taking a short break."

Speaking of breaks, they might have a bad one on their hands here. The teen hadn't seemed to fall hard enough to do any real damage, at least it hadn't looked that way, but the human body was a strange animal.

"Let me check her arm." Carefully unzipping the girl's jacket enough that he could slide his hand down the limb, he found the fracture immediately. Although the bone wasn't protruding from her skin—a good thing—it was pressed right against it. A little more force and it would have come through. The edge felt jagged, though, so it could still break through, if they weren't careful.

The girl was also out cold.

Mira spoke softly to the uninjured girl, while Jack focused on the friend.

"She's still breathing," he said. "Can you get her vitals, while I check her head?" He clicked his boots out of his skis, just like Mira had shown him, and then slid around until he was kneeling beside her shoulder.

Mira nodded, pressing her fingers against the girl's right wrist, while Jack carefully undid the strap to her helmet. He checked it for cracks before running his fingers over her hair, looking for obvious signs of trauma. Her white beanie cap, which had probably been pulled down to hide the unfashionable headgear, lay a short distance away, knocked off by the impact. He couldn't feel any bumps, but he knew that didn't necessarily mean anything. Peeling apart her eyelids one at a time and wishing he had his medical kit, he peered at them to judge pupil size. Equal, and they reacted to light in a way that appeared normal.

Two guys who were evidently with the ski patrol slid to a halt beside them, asking Mira what she had.

"Broken arm at least." She glanced at Jack.

"No contusions on her head that I can see, but I want to stabilize her neck and back just in case."

Her friend stifled a sob. "Is she going to be okay? I wasn't trying to knock her down. I was trying to get my ski loose before I fell. Instead, I made us both fall."

Mira reached over and squeezed her hand, giving the two men a warning look when one of them started to say something. "Of course you didn't. Where are your parents?"

"At—at the lodge. They said we could come ski, but that we had to stick to the easy slopes."

Smart parents.

"And you did what they asked," Mira said. "What's your name?"

"Sandy. And that's Marilyn."

"Okay, Sandy, if you'll go with Hans and help him locate your parents, we'll take care of your friend." Mira stood and helped the girl to her feet, waiting until she'd stopped swaying before saying anything. "Does anything hurt?"

"No. I'm okay."

"Do you feel well enough to ski to the bottom?"

"I—I think so."

The man she'd called Hans patted the terrified girl on the shoulder and gave her an encouraging nod. Then they slowly made their way down the slope, while the other guy went in search of a stretcher and called in the accident, telling the instructors and employees at the top to hold everyone right where they were.

Jack glanced at her. "At least they were wearing helmets. Let's hope she's out because of the pain and not anything else."

"My da...er...the lodge requires all minors to use helmets on the slopes. Her pulse is steady. If we're lucky, she just fainted." She reached her fingers out and smoothed back her hair. "The EMS guys are pretty familiar with the routine up here, they should have something to stabilize her arm."

"I'm beginning to think surfing is a hell of a lot safer."

One curved brow went up. "I can think of a few things that make me think differently. At least you can't drown on a ski slope."

Maybe not, but when her brown eyes met his, looking all soft and warm as she kept her hand protectively on the injured girl's head, he thought it was possible to drown in something other than the ocean.

He shook away the thought.

She's a doctor, Jack. Not someone you want to play around with.

He was glad when a pair of emergency service guys came clomping down the hill, heavy-duty boots making easy work out of the packed snow.

After a quick rundown of her vitals and injuries and explaining what they'd seen, one of the paramedics asked where the girl's parents were.

"We sent her friend and a member of the ski patrol to find them."

In short order, the pair had immobilized the teen's injured arm and done their own assessment of her injuries, coming to the same conclusions as he and Mira had. Then they stabilized her neck and removed her skis before loading her onto a blue stretcher with a metal pull bar attached to it. The girl started to come to, moaning as her eyes fluttered open.

Mira leaned close and whispered to her.

The sight made a pang go through his chest. If he and Paula had had any kids, is that how she would've looked as she comforted them?

Not the time, Jack.

He cleared his throat. "They're going to pull her down the hill?"

"That's the safest way. It's hard to keep your balance on the snow, if you haven't noticed." The right side of her mouth curved slightly, as if she was fighting a smile.

"Oh, I noticed all right." In fact, he was having a little trouble keeping his balance right now, and it had nothing to do with skiing. He felt like the wind had been knocked from his lungs the second he'd realized she was a doctor. He was still struggling to catch his breath fifteen minutes later.

She stood and went over to retrieve the girl's

hat and skis. "I'll bring these down with me," she told the men. "Hopefully they've located her folks. I want to be on hand if something changes."

"Sure thing, Mira." One of the medical workers threw her a quick smile.

It seemed everyone knew her around these parts.

The paramedics started down the hill, leaving them to follow.

"Do you want to walk down or ski?"

"At the rate I go, it's probably faster to walk." He took the girl's skis from her and lumped them together with his, tucking them under his arm with his poles.

Together, they trudged down the bunny slope, staying a few yards behind the rescue team. His mind couldn't help wandering back to her instructions on how to maneuver with his skis and how her words had yielded much better results than the lessons her ex—the professional—had given him.

Wanting to show off for the pretty doctor, Jack?

Self-preservation was more like it. Something he should probably remember. Because the fact that she was a doctor was all the more reason he should avoid her for the rest of his stay. If his coach were here, he'd be calling for a time-out and hauling Jack's ass off the playing field.

And the man would be right. Injured players should remain on the sidelines until they had time to heal.

Yeah? Well, he'd had four damn years. How much longer would it take?

Some players never recovered. Maybe he was one of them. He could just throw in the towel right now.

His body gave a quick tug of irritation, one that grew when Mira glanced back at him with a smile. "Keeping up okay?"

Oh, he could keep up just fine. He balled his hands into fists when his mind immediately headed into more dangerous territory. Of Mira saying those words under very different circum-stances.

Sidelines, Jack, remember?

Thankfully, they reached the bottom of the slope, and he had other things to occupy his mind, like the small crowd that had gathered near the door of the lodge, and the woman in a pink parka rushing forward to meet the EMS guys as they headed for the pick-up site where their truck was probably parked. Forced to stop, the guys lifted the stretcher just as he and Mira arrived.

Habit made him start toward the group to brief the girl's parents, but Mira beat him to it, smoothly maneuvering right into the center of the gathering. Besides, he wasn't here with his football team. This was her gig, not his.

He could see her gesturing as she explained the situation, but he couldn't hear the words. Whatever she said, it seemed to have the right effect. People started to move away until all that was left were a man and a woman who looked like they were in their early fifties—Marilyn's parent's probably—standing near the stretcher. Jack debated slipping through the glass doors of the lodge and escaping while he could, while Mira's attention was fixed on something else.

Coward's way out. He'd decided four years ago that he wasn't going that route ever again. He'd lost his head in a bottle for a while after his wife's death. Once he'd picked himself up off the bathroom floor after a particularly bad hangover, he'd decided to live a life Paula would be proud of rather than throwing it away in a booze-filled haze. He obviously wasn't there yet—this temporary exile and the sleep aids were proof of that.

What he needed was something to take his mind off himself for a few hours.

His eyes slid back to Mira, whose glossy hair showed beneath her cap as she leaned over the stretcher to talk to the injured girl once more.

Nope. No matter how tempting that might be, it wasn't smart. He needed something light and easy. Something other than skiing with pretty women.

Large black letters from a flyer taped to the door of the lodge caught his attention:

Not a Ski Fan?

Ha, you could say that. He continued reading.

Check out Silver Pass's other exciting offerings.

The bullet points proceeded to list things like evening sleigh rides, trips down the mountains on inner tubes, gondola lifts that boasted spectacular views, and even snowmobile rentals.

The snowmobiles sounded interesting. Maybe even a little bit like jet skis.

He pulled out his smartphone to store the number in his address book.

"The gondola ride is a lot of fun. And there's only room for two in each car."

A sultry voice came from just over his left shoulder. Not Mira's, since she was still over by the stretcher.

He turned around and found a brunette with darkly penciled brows that matched the carefully modulated tones of her voice. Overdone. Whispering of desperation. And when the woman smiled, nothing happened to the skin around her eyes.

Botox.

He'd thought of Mira as a professional snow bunny when he'd first met her, but her sparkling eyes and sunny disposition had dashed his suspicions away. This woman, however...

Swallowing, he nodded. "I'll keep that in mind, thank you."

She took a step closer, her jacket pulling tight

across her breasts. "Did I overhear someone say that you're a doctor?"

Oh, Lord. Not what he wanted to deal with right now.

Why was it that a quick fling with Mira appealed to him, despite its dangers, while the thought of spending the night with this woman just left him cold? He didn't want to hurt her feelings—if they hadn't already been paralyzed by the overzealous needle of her surgeon.

"I am. Just here for a couple of days' R&R." Okay, a couple of days was on the verge of being a lie, since he still had three weeks left of his vacation.

"That's enough time to squeeze in a fun activity or two, isn't it? It'll be a tight fit, but it would be well worth the effort."

She said the words with a completely straight face, but she had to know how they sounded.

Hell. He was surprised *she* wasn't listed on that flier as one of the lodge's alternate activities, along with her name, phone number, and measurements. And that she promised a tight fit.

"Well—"

Mira suddenly appeared beside them, looking from one to the other. "I wondered where you went." She glanced at the advertisement and then the phone in his hand. "Planning something fun?"

"Thinking about it. Did Marilyn get off okay?"

"She's on her way to the hospital right now."

The brunette quirked a brow. Wow, maybe there wasn't as much happy juice in her face as he'd thought. "Girlfriend?" she asked, her voice not quite as sultry as it had been.

He wanted to say yes, just to get rid of her without having to be rude. Would Mira kill him? He could always explain later.

"She's—"

"Definitely a girlfriend. And you are?" Mira wrapped her hands around his right bicep, giving it a quick squeeze as if to say she knew he was in a tight spot.

Squeeze. Tight spot. Well the woman might not have done anything for him with those words, but Mira's touch was definitely doing something to his gut. It clenched, one muscle group at a time, until his whole abdomen was a mass of tension.

"Well, why didn't you say so?" The brunette tossed her head.

Mira's hand ventured from his arm, sliding low across his back until it curved around his left side. She left a trail of heat in her wake that he felt even through his coat. "He's too nice. Women get the wrong idea all the time."

Evidently she didn't have any of the same reservations about hurting the woman's feelings as he did, because she continued. "So did you get the number for that sleigh-ride company, Jack, or what?"

"I was just doing that."

"Good." Her glance shot to the brunette. "Thanks for keeping him company for me. I've got it from here."

With a strangled sound the woman wheeled around and then jerked open the door to the lodge before disappearing inside.

The breath he hadn't realized he'd been holding whistled out through his teeth as relief swept over him. "How did you know?"

She let go of his side and lifted her hand to pat his cheek. "Your face is about as red as the walls in the dining hall." She laughed. "And she's a regular. She comes on to all the men."

There was a bitter edge to her words.

So much for thinking she'd singled him out. Ouch. The punch to his ego stung.

"So I wasn't in any real danger."

"I didn't say that. She's dangerous all right."

As much as he tried to school his face into a blank slate, a smile crept up from somewhere inside him. "How do you know I don't thrive on danger?"

"Do you? I didn't take you for the type."

There it was again. That quick one-two to his pride. "I might surprise you."

"Really? In that case, I think you owe me a sleigh ride. For bailing you out of what could have been an awkward situation. Especially if her husband had found out."

"She's married?" Maybe he did owe her something.

"Aren't they all?"

He wouldn't know. He hadn't been on the dating circuit since he'd met Paula. "I guess you wouldn't accept a simple thank-you."

"I would, but I couldn't promise I'd bail you out a second time. If her being married doesn't stop her, do you really think me saying I'm your girlfriend is going to scare her off? But if she knows you not only *have* a girlfriend but that you're *happy* with that girlfriend, she'll probably leave you alone."

Jack's head was spinning, partly at the audacity of married women propositioning men who were taken and partly just because of the clean crisp scent of the woman at his side. It reminded him of frosty days and mocha-filled nights. He leaned in closer. "Did you just have coffee?"

Why he asked that he had no idea.

She blinked at him in surprise. She could match that look and raise it. His face heated again.

"I just ate a coffee-flavored candy."

"Sorry. I think my brain is misfiring over what just happened."

"You've never been propositioned by a married woman before?" Her voice was shocked, like it was something that happened all the time.

"Never. If you were married, would you do it? Proposition someone who wasn't your husband?"

"Oh, but I'm not married." Although light and delivered with a smile, her words contained a hint of darkness. Because of her ex? Had he slept with Mrs. Botox or something?

He decided to change the subject entirely. "So this sleigh ride. Is it worth going on alone?"

"Um, yeah, but if she finds out you're planning on going solo, she's going to show up and invite herself along for the ride."

He glanced through the glass to see that the brunette in question was indeed eyeing them while sipping on something boozy that looked like it had a tiny plastic ski sticking out of it. He guessed ski resorts didn't want little umbrellas reminding people they could be in a tropical paradise instead. "As much as I never thought I'd say it, would you mind going with me? To ward off trouble…" He wasn't sure that "warding off" trouble was the right way to put it. Because it sure felt like he was busy cultivating it at the moment.

"No problem. I haven't been on a sleigh ride in ages, actually."

So her ex hadn't taken her on one? Maybe they'd had fun in other ways.

Something that made his jaw tense.

She grabbed his hand. "And now for my last good deed until our sleigh ride." She hauled him through the door and paraded him right in front of Mrs. Botox, their hands firmly joined. They were about halfway to the receptionist's desk when she turned to grin at him and then promptly plowed into an older man who stepped into her path.

"Oh, I'm sorry." She turned around. "I didn't see…"

Her voice died away, and her face drained of all its color as she looked up at the man she'd just run into. She let go of Jack's hand in a rush.

The stranger's brows came together, and his eyes narrowed as he studied Jack and then Mira. Then he addressed her, saying, "I think you have some explaining to do."

Her arms went around her waist, and she drew in a shaky breath. "Daddy, what are you doing here?"

CHAPTER FOUR

MIRA TRIED TO give off an appearance of calm.

But her heart was ticking at an alarming pace, and she was aware of Jack standing just behind her. He had to be wondering what the hell was going on.

He wasn't the only one. She was pretty much wondering the same thing.

Why was her father here? He rarely put in an appearance at the lodge these days. And he wasn't exactly what she would call "involved" in her life any more. Although much of that was her own fault. Even when he'd tried to get close over the past several years while she'd been at med school, she'd tended to pull away. Her mom had let his infidelity go, why couldn't she?

"Well?" he said, evidently waiting for that explanation he'd asked for.

She lifted her chin, refusing to act the part of

the meek little girl he'd once carried around on his shoulders. "You want an explanation? Maybe you should ask Robert for one."

"Robert, what's he got to do with this?" He looked genuinely puzzled.

Gulping, she scrambled to figure out what else he could be talking about. She figured her ex had called her father—like he'd hinted he would do—to cry on his shoulder or ask him to intervene on his behalf. And that her dad had hightailed it up to Silver Pass to give her hell. Okay, so if that wasn't the case, it could only mean he was asking for an explanation about why she was holding hands with a strange man. She glanced back at Jack and blew out a breath at the grim expression on his face. Her dad wasn't the only one asking some mental questions. Better get the introductions out of the way.

"Sorry. I'll talk to you about Robert later." She motioned Jack closer. "Daddy, this is Jack Perry. He's the team doctor for the Texas Hawks. He helped out with an accident on the slopes a few minutes ago."

"The Hawks? I'm impressed." He stuck out a hand. "Nice to meet you."

He proceeded to grill Jack on his opinion of this team or that and what he thought of Texas and Colorado's chances for making it to the play-offs next year.

She felt bad about throwing Jack to Papa Wolf, but if anything could distract her dad it was football. It would at least give her time to think before the subject eventually swung back to her and what she feared would be the subject *du jour*: why she was holding hands with a man who wasn't her fiancé, team doctor or no team doctor.

Not that she owed him any explanations after the way he'd treated her mom. But, still, it would be awkward to tell him to mind his own business in front of Jack.

So, what could she tell him?

How about: Jack was blind, and she was helping him find the reception desk.

Nope, that wouldn't work, since the Hawks probably wouldn't hire a blind physician.

That left… Yeah. She was drawing a complete blank.

"Mira?" Her dad's voice dragged her from her thoughts.

Her head came up. "Sorry?"

"I invited Jack to have dinner with us tonight at eight. Hope that was okay?"

She couldn't have been any more shocked if her dad had suddenly started doing the chicken dance in front of everyone in the crowded lobby. She'd expected a scene and had gotten a dinner invitation instead. Although with her dad, it normally came out sounding more like an ultimatum. "No, of course I don't mind, if it's all right with him."

Jack glanced at the lobby, and Mira noted that Predator in Pink was still watching them closely. "It's fine with me," he said.

Did this make two or three dates with guy number five? She was supposed to be moving on to the next eligible bachelor and then the next. Her gaze slid back to the woman across the room. Yeah, she so did not want to become that. Maybe she should stop being so anxious to zip from man to man.

Besides, she and Jack hadn't actually had their first date yet. Right? Because the hot chocolate didn't count, and the ski lesson had been interrupted by the rescue on the slope, so that didn't count either.

And the sleigh ride?

Hmm, that could definitely be classified as a date. Which would officially mark the end of their association.

Her father gave her a quick hug. "Do you want to ask Robert to come as well?"

"Robert?" Nothing like her emotions swinging from relief to panic. She was going to have to break the news to her father. But not now. Not in front of Jack. "I'm sure he's busy with lessons."

"Okay, if you're sure." He smiled as he released her. "You know, that boy's future father-in-law is the owner of this joint. I could probably pull a few strings and have him let off early."

Jack visibly stiffened beside her. "It was nice meeting you," he said to her father. "But I need to turn in my equipment and get cleaned up. Thank you for the dinner invitation."

The last thing she wanted was to be left alone with her father. "I can go with you to the rental kiosk, if you don't remember where it is."

"I remember. Thanks for your…help earlier. I think I've got it from here."

That must be one of the man's favorite phrases. How many times did that make now? Three?

About as many times as she'd been with him. Well, that was just great.

Waiting until Jack was three or four strides away, she raised her voice just enough for the woman across the room to hear. "Don't forget about making the reservation for the sleigh ride. Believe me, you won't want to miss it."

Now, why had she said that? Maybe because it stung that he couldn't seem to get away from her fast enough.

Jack stopped in his tracks for a second or two before throwing her a look that was filled with lazy amusement totally at odds with his abrupt departure. And when his voice came back, it was much lower than hers had been. "Believe me, I haven't forgotten."

A shiver went over her at the dark intensity of his words. She glanced sharply up at her father to see if he'd noticed, but he seemed lost in his own world at the moment. Once Jack had gone through the door she turned her attention back to her father, bracing herself for a confrontation. Better to just tell him the truth and get it over with.

"Dad, I have something to tell you," she began.

"I have something to tell you as well. Actually, I wanted to ask you for a favor. It's why I came up here today."

She gulped. A favor? "Is it about Robert?"

If he was going to ask her to give her ex a second chance, she might just blow her top. One cheater asking her to forgive and forget the transgressions of another cheater? Not hardly. Especially when one of the women Robert had cheated with was standing on the other side of the room.

"It's not about Robert, it's about…" He focused on her face. "Is everything okay between the two of you?"

She frowned, trying to figure out exactly what was going on.

"Things are a little complicated." *A little, Mira? Really?* "Anyway, what's this about a favor?"

A sliver of worry went through her as she noticed for the first time the taut lines of his face.

If he hadn't come here because of her breakup, then why had he come?

"Not here. Let's go back to my office, Mirry."

She hadn't heard that nickname in forever. The sliver grew to the size of a stake. "Dad, is something wrong? Oh God, is it Mom?"

"No, your mother's fine. I spoke with her this morning."

Mira's eyes widened. He had? More alarm bells went off as he crossed the honey-planked flooring and headed for the door that led to a different wing of the lodge, one that wasn't open to the public. She followed him, winding through the narrow corridors until they reached the small annex where his office and the business areas were housed. Once the door shut behind them, he motioned her to one of the leather wingback chairs across from his desk.

She dropped into it, the creak of leather matching that of her nerves. "Daddy?"

All the differences of the past several years seemed to vanish as her unease continued to grow.

Instead of going behind the desk to face her, he

went to the bar on the left and got down a tumbler from the open wooden shelves above the liquor bottles and dumped a few cubes of ice into it. He stared at the selection of alcohol for a long time—as if he'd never seen it before—and finally grabbed a decanter, uncapping it and pouring himself a healthy amount. He rarely drank, and only kept the liquor here for VIP meetings and gatherings.

He took a good-sized swig then sighed and added another splash of whatever was in the decanter. "I know I haven't done right by you and your mother. I've often wished I could go back and change some things, but I can't."

He turned around to face her, leaning against the counter and taking another sip from his glass. As if realizing his oversight, he frowned. "Do you want something?"

It was probably better if she didn't have anything this early, but she suddenly felt the need to brace herself for whatever he was about to say. "Maybe a little red wine?"

He fixed her a glass then brought it over and

handed it to her before dragging the other chair around so it faced her.

She clenched her glass. Something was definitely wrong. "Are you ill?"

"No, Mirry, but it might be better if I were."

Her heart squeezed. "Don't say that," she whispered. Suddenly the years she'd wasted being angry with him flew by at an alarming rate, dropping her into the here and now. She set her untouched drink onto the marble-topped table next to her.

He smiled and took another drink, the ice clinking against his glass. "That comment surprises me, to be honest."

"We might have our differences, but you're still my father."

"Yes, I am. And something has come up that's made me aware of all the mistakes I made with you. With your mom. It has made me want to do all I can to make things right and to not…" he gave a visible swallow "…repeat those mistakes with anyone else."

"What is it?"

"Stella's pregnant."

Stella. It took her a minute to put a face with a name.

Paramour number six? Or was it seven? Pregnant?

Mira would have asked if he was sure, but from the redness in his eyes and the unsteadiness of the hand holding the drink she'd say he was dead certain. Instead, she ventured, "Are you happy about that?"

He held her gaze for a long time before nodding. "I screwed up with you. With your mother. Maybe I can learn from those mistakes and do a better job this time around."

He wasn't dying. Her mom wasn't dying. That's all that mattered. She stood and went over to him, taking his drink and setting it on the table behind him. Kneeling beside the chair, she put her arms around him and laid her head on his chest, feeling a love and affection she hadn't felt in a very long time. "I'm happy for you, Daddy. Really happy. If I know Mom, she is too."

His hand came up to stroke her hair. "I plan to marry Stella. I came to ask you for your blessing."

She leaned back to look at him. He'd surprised her yet again. Her father of old would have simply declared his intentions and dared her to say a word against it. It was one of the reasons they hadn't reconciled over the years. He'd acted like the world was his to own...to possess at will.

And yet now he wanted her blessing. If she wanted to blast him with accusations, now was the time. Only she didn't want to.

"You have it, Daddy. Of course you do."

"I know I haven't even walked you down the aisle yet, but I want to ask if you'd do me the honor of standing beside me as I take my vows."

A wave of emotion rolled over her, bringing with it a prickling at the backs of her eyelids. She blinked it away as best she could. "Is that okay with Stella?"

"Yes. She wants to meet you. I called your mom as well, to ask her permission. She told me to ask you, and that she'd support your decision whatever it was." He paused. "Stella's a wonderful woman, Mirry. I want to do right by her. And by you this time. This is the only way I know how."

"Then, of course, I'll stand beside you. I'd be happy to."

A ragged sigh went past her ear. "Thank you. It means the world to me."

She squeezed him tight before leaning over to kiss his grizzled cheek. She stood and took a step back, noticing for the first time the heavy streaks of gray in his still thick hair. When had that happened? When she'd been too busy with her anger to look directly at him?

"I love you, Daddy."

"I love you too, princess." The man who'd always seemed larger than life to Mira dragged his fist across his eyes then stood as well. "Now, what's this about you and Robert?"

It was tempting to just put it off, to pretend that things were fine, but her dad had been honest and real with her for the first time in years. She could do no less.

"I broke our engagement."

He stood there silent for a long time before saying anything. "What happened?"

Honesty, Mira.

Although maybe she could put a little spin on

that honesty so she wouldn't mar his moment of happiness or endanger the tentative bridge they'd just built between them.

"It just wasn't working."

"I'm sorry. Is there anything I can do?"

"About that? Not a thing." She nodded toward her untouched glass. "But I think I've changed my mind about my drink. If you have something festive in that wine cooler of yours, like champagne, I vote we pop the cork and toast to your good fortune. And to my new baby brother or sister."

The first snowfall since his arrival met Jack as he stepped into the lobby for his "date."

Why he'd booked that sleigh ride he had no idea. Maybe because Mira had reminded him again at dinner two nights ago with her father—which he'd found he couldn't get out of, no matter how badly he'd wanted to. He'd had no idea Mira was a doctor, let alone that her father owned the whole damn resort. Neither of them had mentioned her ex fiancé. In fact, they'd both seemed pretty set on avoiding that whole subject during their meal.

Did her father even know?

He'd gotten very little sleep last night. His bottle of pills had whispered to him from the drawer of the nightstand, but he'd ignored it. And the dreams had come back with a vengeance.

As tired as he was, the last thing Jack wanted was to get involved in some huge family drama. He'd had enough of that to last him a lifetime. The blame game had made the rounds after his wife's death with every finger in her family—including his own—pointed directly at his chest, where there was still a gaping hole that no amount of shoveling could fill.

Jabbing his fists into the pockets of his dark slacks, he stared out the window at the whisper-soft flakes dancing in the night breeze, the outside lights making them glimmer and sparkle as they made their way to earth. There were a few footprints across the snow, but for the most part the new layer stretched across the acreage of the resort like a blanket. The walkways had yet to be shoveled. Mira said the sleigh would pull up at the far edge of the drive, a hundred yards or so from the front entrance of the main building. There was no sign of the sleigh, or of Mira, for that matter.

Maybe he could just go back to his room and try to get some rest.

As if hearing his thoughts, the far door opened, and the woman herself appeared. His breath caught in his chest. Unlike her puffy white ski jacket, which did a good job of concealing her figure, tonight she wore a long wool coat that skimmed her body and almost reached her ankles. Open at the front, it gave a tantalizing glimpse of a shiny green top tucked into slim black pants that hugged her hips and legs. A belt of silver metallic links encircled her waist, the ends trailing down her left thigh. She made her way over to him, shrugging her way out of the coat as she did and draping it over her left arm.

"I wasn't sure if you'd be outside yet or not," she said.

"Our ride isn't here, so I thought I'd wait by the door and watch for it." No reason to tell her he'd been about to make his escape.

Her subtle scent drifted up, a melding of vanilla and pine, a combination that wound around him. His exhaustion suddenly vanished.

"You should have worn boots," she said, glancing down at where his loafers peeked from beneath the bottom edge of his pants legs.

"I didn't bring any. Just the rental snow boots."

Her brows went up. "Really? You live in Texas, and you didn't at least bring some cowboy boots?"

"I don't own any."

"Wow, no boots. At all."

"My recreational choices normally involve water. No need for boots. Or even shoes."

Her lips twisted in a wry smile that made her eyes sparkle. "A man who prefers to go shoeless, huh? You wouldn't survive long up here. Not if you wanted to keep those toes."

He peered down at her feet and noted that, unlike him, she did own boots, but these had a tall chunky heel to them. "And those don't look any more practical than my own footwear."

That got a laugh out of her. "I know, aren't they great? I don't get much of a chance to wear them in my profession."

He came back to earth with a bump. That's right. She worked here. *Dr.* Miranda Dupris. "You don't have to entertain me, you know. I'm sure that's not part of your job description."

"Oh, it's the best part. Fraternize with all the handsome bachelors and make sure they're happy."

He shot her a look, only to have her grin again. "I'm kidding. I'll leave that to your buddy from the other day."

Mrs. Botox. Thankfully he hadn't seen her since they'd parted ways in the lobby, despite Mira's warning. Even in the dining room over the last two evenings there'd been no sign of her. But during his dinner with Mira and her father the blonde who had waved to Mira several days ago had made her way over to their table and given Mira a quick squeeze. Then she'd hugged Mira's dad.

As she'd said goodbye a few minutes later, she'd thrown one last wink Mira's way. "Still five, I see."

"It's not quite five. Ask me again in a couple of days," Mira had replied.

It was the same number they'd tossed back and forth the other day, when he'd wondered if they were meeting up for a drink or something. Neither of them expanded on the comment and after that cryptic exchange the blonde had flounced away, waving off attempts to get her to stay and eat dinner with them. "I'm going on a quick hike to work on my own resolution."

Only afterwards did he notice that Mira had made no effort to introduce her to him.

Mira touched his arm, drawing him back to the present. "Do you want to head down the path to wait?"

"Are you going to be okay in those boots?"

"As okay as you'll be okay in your shoes." Her gaze slanted over him. "You look good, by the way."

"So do you." It was true. For once she was hatless, her red hair flowing over her shoulders where it complemented the green of her blouse. Her warm brown eyes seemed darker than usual, although that could be the result of make-up or something. Whatever the cause, the woman was a knockout. And with her heels on, those legs of hers looked endless, her chin coming right to his shoulder level. Unusual for him. At five feet five, the top of Paula's head, even in her tallest shoes, had barely come to the middle of his chest.

Why was he suddenly comparing the two? Turning away, he picked up his leather jacket from across a nearby chair and shrugged into it, zipping it halfway up his chest. Putting on his armor? He forced a lightness to his voice that he didn't feel. "You sure the sleigh company is going to send someone in this snow?"

"They usually do. If not, we can go for a walk instead."

"With your boots and my shoes."

She tossed her head. "Why not? It's just a little snow." When she went to put her own coat on, he took it from her and held it out so she could slide her arms inside. His fingers brushed the warmth of her neck as he set it on her shoulders, the sensation of smooth silky skin branding itself on his senses.

He forced his hands back into his pockets. "Shall we?"

They strolled out the door and started down the

pathway as the snow fell around them. It wasn't deep on the sidewalk, more like a dusting, but Mira pulled the collar of her coat up around her neck anyway.

"Are you going to be cold without a hat?"

"I have one in my pocket. Besides, they have blankets in the sleigh that we can hunker down under."

Images of the two of them snuggled together beneath a pile of blankets came out of nowhere. And hell if they weren't followed up by other images of what the parts hidden beneath the blankets could do.

This was *so* not a good idea. He'd known if from the second she suggested they go together. Maybe he should start hoping that sleigh didn't come after all.

He zipped his jacket even higher, though it wasn't in reaction to the cold that was trickling down his spine but because of a wave of warmth he couldn't fight off.

It had been far too long since he'd been with someone. Maybe he should have taken Mrs. Botox up on her offer. Except he wouldn't hit on

Mrs. Anything. As messed up as he was these days, he still didn't believe in that.

"How long is this ride, anyway?" A question he should have asked at the reception desk when he'd booked this little excursion. But he'd been too relieved at having survived dinner with Mira and her dad and too busy wondering if she'd told her father that the infamous future son-in-law was now an ex. How many of those did she have, anyway? He'd seen her with a couple of different guys when he'd arrived. Since he and Paula had been childhood sweethearts, he'd never been down the date-'em-and-leave-'em path. He'd had a couple of one-night stands since his wife's death, but that was the extent of it. And it had been over a year since his last rendezvous.

One of Mira's feet slid for a second, and Jack put his hand out to steady her.

"Sorry," she said. "Guess I laughed at your choice of footwear a little too soon, since you're doing better in yours than I am in mine."

"Here." Holding out his elbow to her, he wasn't sure if he was elated or disturbed when she took him up on the offer and looped her arm through his and hugged close. It was too much like what she'd done when rescuing him from Mrs. Botox's advances.

And he liked the feel of her next to him a little too much. It felt warm and companionable. Just like Mira herself.

The woman didn't talk nonstop, like he'd been expecting. And he found himself wishing she did. He liked the sound of her voice.

How the hell did he even know what her voice sounded like?

He did, though. He could hear it in his head. Hear the words they'd exchanged since their first meeting less than a week ago.

Was that all it had been?

"We should be good here," she murmured.

"Good?"

She nodded at something next to them. A signpost with rustic hand-painted arrows pointed in various directions. The top arrow said, "Sleigh Ride Pick-up Point Here."

"How long has your dad owned this place?"

"He built it. He inherited the land from his grandfather and decided to do something with it. He and my mom lived in a little cabin a mile or two down the road before he decided to build the resort. He's tried to preserve the natural beauty and disturb the surrounding area as little as possible." She let go of his arm and stuffed her hands in the pockets of her long coat, shifting her weight slightly away from him.

"I'd say he succeeded. It's a restful place. Did you spend your childhood here?"

"Until I got out of high school."

She didn't offer any other explanation than that, but her voice had hardened slightly. Better not to press her for anything more on that subject.

A musical *chink-chink-chink-chink* sounded in the distance, growing closer. A minute or two later a large cream-colored horse came into view, pulling a sleigh that looked like it had come straight out of a Christmas song, complete with sleigh bells. With shiny black side panels, the sled sat atop gracefully curved silver runners. The interior was lined in red velvet and the whole vehicle gave the impression of an "S" that had been tilted onto its side—the driver sitting up front on a high plush bench, while a second seat sat further back and much lower to the ground. The passenger area had a very private appearance that didn't do anything for his already taut nerves. And true to Mira's words, a pile of folded blankets sat next to the driver.

The horse snorted and shook its head, making the bells attached to his harness jingle again. Mira moved over to the animal and stroked its neck. "How are you doing, Patsy?"

Patsy? The huge animal looked nothing like its name.

The driver tied the reins to a bar on the front of the sleigh and clambered down from his seat. "Hello, Mira. It's been a while since you've ridden with us. Patsy's missed you."

"I know. I've missed her too. And you." She glanced back at Jack. "This is Norman, our driver. Norm, this is Jack Perry, one of the resort's guests. He's never ridden on a sleigh before. In fact, there are quite a few things he hasn't done before."

Jack's neck and face grew hot at the way she'd said it, as if he were an inexperienced teenager being let out into the world for the first time.

Actually, that might not be too far from the truth. It had been a while since he'd let *himself* out into the world. And that hadn't even been his idea. He had his coach to thank for this awkward little mountaintop excursion.

"Nice to meet you." Norm—an older man with a close-cropped silver beard and matching hair—reached out to shake his hand. His top hat and black wool coat gave him a formal air that went well with the sleigh. "If you two are ready…? Patsy's glad to be out of that barn and is raring to go."

The man then reached up to his seat, snagged two thick plaid blankets and handed them to Jack. "It gets chilly back there—better bundle up." He smiled. "Mira used to look like a baby polar bear when she was young, she'd wrap up in so many layers. She'd fall asleep in the back and let us pull her and Ellory all over the place."

Perfect. He'd been hoping to ignore the whole hunker-beneath-the-blanket thing. He covered it up by asking, "Ellory?"

Mira came over to stand beside them. "The

woman who stopped by our table at dinner. She's a good friend of mine."

That's why her name sounded familiar.

Giving the harness a quick check, Norm said, "Ellory came out to say hello to me a few days ago. I didn't realize she was back in town."

"She's here for a visit. I'm trying to talk her into staying."

Jack shifted the blankets to the other hand. "She's also the one who gestured she'd meet you in five minutes when we were in the bar, right?"

"Five…?"

Jack couldn't be sure if it was just a trick of the old-fashioned gas streetlamp, but her face seemed to grow pink, the tip of her nose taking on a warm glow. "Yes, that was her."

Before he had a chance to wonder if something was wrong, the driver gestured to the back seat. "Climb aboard." He tweaked Mira on the nose. "You want me to take the scenic route up by the silver mines?"

"Would you? I'm sure Jack'll want to see them."

"For you? Anything. I'll let you point out

the sights, since you know them as well as I do by now."

The scenic route. He had no idea what that meant, but had a feeling it was a whole lot longer than the traditional route.

The snow had let up as he climbed into the back of the sleigh and then held out a hand to Mira and helped her up. The velvet seats were warm and inviting against the chill of the air. "Are these heated?"

Mira took the blankets from him and shook them out, placing them over their laps. "Mmm-hmm. Norm installed them. They're powered with a rechargeable battery pack beneath the seat." She snuggled deep, pulling one of the blankets up to her chin. "Comfortable?"

With the seats or with the company? At the moment he couldn't really answer that. Despite his misgivings about coming on this little outing, he felt himself relax in a way he hadn't in quite a while. It could be the lack of sleep, or it could just be from having a pretty woman sitting next to him. He could just glimpse a patch of stars through a break in the heavy cloud cover, and although the little pinpoints didn't throw off much light, the streetlamps made up for them, providing a nice glow that ran down the path as far as he could see.

Norm clucked to the horse and turned her around in the small cul-de-sac, and then they were on their way, the metal runners making a slicing sound as they cut across the frozen earth.

The back of the vehicle was clearly built for romance and late nights under the stars. The walls surrounding them forced them close enough together that their shoulders touched.

Mira rested her head against the back of the seat with a sigh. "It's been ages since I've been out on the sleigh. It always used to put me to sleep."

Funny, because, despite his earlier thoughts, the last thing Jack felt like doing right now was sleeping. "How's he going to find his way in the dark?"

"The paths are all lit, even the back ones, and the resort has its own plow to keep the snow from getting too deep on these throughways." She angled her head to the side so she was facing him. "Thanks for letting me tag along."

A smile tugged at one corner of his mouth. "I should be thanking you again for bailing me out of an awkward situation."

Not that the one he was in now was any less awkward.

"Mmm, well, you saved me from dining alone with my dad. Once you get him talking about football, that's all he wants to discuss. That lets me off the hook."

That surprised him. The two of them had seemed close. "Do you not get along?"

"We haven't for a long time, but things are changing." She sighed and turned toward the front again. "I'm hoping we can make a fresh start."

He shifted to his right so he could see her better in the shadows. "You didn't tell him about your breakup that night at dinner. Did you let him know later?"

The sleigh rounded a corner, pressing him against her for a second or two, before heading down a slightly darker path. He didn't try to move away. With their heads close together, as well as the shared space beneath the heavy blankets, they could have been children whispering in the dark. Only Mira was no child. The rise and fall of her breasts as she gave another sigh reinforced that fact. "I told him that first night, although I just shared the bare essentials. Daddy always liked Robert, so I didn't want to disillusion him."

"About your ex?"

She nodded. "And the reasons we broke up. I'm afraid telling my father about that will reopen some old wounds between us."

Had she cheated on her fiancé? Somehow he didn't think so. From the way she'd talked about Mrs. Botox and the men the woman targeted, Jack couldn't help but think Mira was cut from very different cloth.

"Your ex was an idiot for not wanting to work things out."

That got a laugh out of her. "I agree with the idiot part, but it was actually me who didn't want to work it out. Why bother when you obviously don't have what it takes to make someone happy."

Have what it took. Was she kidding? He was

sitting here trying to think of anything but the warm, soft body hidden beneath those blankets and how easy it would be to simply lean forward and kiss her.

He swallowed, trying to rein in his wayward thoughts, but it wasn't easy. "I had no idea there were silver mines up here. Is that where the town gets its name?"

"Yes. This whole area is riddled with them. It was a big industry once upon a time. The best thing my grandfather ever did was make sure he held onto the mineral rights, even though my dad has no interest in mining the mountain."

Another turn had the wind blowing right at them. Mira shivered and gripped the covers tighter.

"Cold?"

"I'm okay. The breeze is just chilly."

Before he could stop himself, Jack slipped his arm around her shoulders and tugged her against his body, pulling the blankets up around both of them. "Better?"

"Mmm. Much." She laid her head on his shoulder, her arm going across his abdomen and making him all too aware that if she shifted it four inches lower, an uncomfortable reality was going to meet her.

He closed his eyes and let the cold of the outside air flow deep into his lungs in an effort to cool himself from the inside out. Instead, he found himself absorbing the feel of her, and thinking about how long it had been since he'd felt a woman against him in anything other than a quick round of sex.

This felt a whole lot more intimate than that because he was aware of Mira on more than just a physical level.

She surrounded him. Her scent. Her touch. The sound of her breathing. It was all right there. Coaxing him closer. A siren's song that was growing harder and harder to resist, even though he knew he should.

The snow-covered path helped muffled the clip-clop of Patsy's hooves, but the jingling of the bells on her harness sounded with each footfall.

And Mira was right. The whole experience was hypnotic. Soothing.

"Jack?"

"Yep?" He laid his cheek against the top of her head.

To keep the wind from hitting it.

Sure, buddy. Keep on telling yourself that.

"I think I'm supposed to be giving you Norm's tourist spiel. What do you want to know?"

He chuckled. "I'm too comfortable right now to really care." As soon as he said the words he knew it was true. He also knew it was the last thing he should have admitted.

Instead of kicking him away from her in horror, she murmured, "That's good. Because I'm too comfortable to play tour guide."

"We're even, then."

He reached up to smooth a strand of her hair that tickled his nose. Then, instead of dropping his hand back to his side, he allowed it to trail down the side of her face, touching the cool softness of her flesh for the first time. Not really, but it was the first time he'd purposely touched her for a reason other than being hauled up off his ass or letting her pretend to be something she wasn't.

She could be, though. The insidious thought whispered through his mind just as his fingers reached her chin, his thumb strumming across the little indentation he found there. And hell if she didn't have the silkiest skin known to man-kind.

Her sigh let him know she wasn't unhappy with what he was doing. If anything, she nestled closer, her hand splaying over his abs and send-ing a heady wave of warmth rolling down to his groin. This was a dangerous game to be playing in the back of a sleigh. A literal one-horse open sleigh.

His lips twisted. Scratch that. This was a dan-gerous game to be playing anywhere…with any-one…although, since the vehicle was in motion, there was almost no likelihood of having a po-lice officer flash his spotlight on them, warning them to move along.

He explored the line of her jaw, his eyes travel-ing up to the seat in front of them for a second, but Norm and the horse had their attention fo-cused on where they were going rather than on what was happening behind them. And there was no rear-view mirror that he could see.

No one would ever know.

No one would see if he... He slid his palm across the side of her throat, allowing it to rest there for a moment to gauge her response.

She didn't move. He swallowed, the need to do something crazy growing by the second.

It had to be sleep deprivation.

Still, he raised his head to look down at her. Her eyes were closed, her lips barely parted as she breathed. If not for the frantic beat of her pulse against his skin he might think she was asleep. But she wasn't. His thumb went to the bottom of her chin and exerted a slight upward pressure. As if she knew what was coming, her head tilted back to the perfect angle. Her eyelids parted, warm brown irises meeting his gaze. In their depths he saw the answer to his unspoken question.

She wouldn't stop him.

He murmured her name into the cold night. Softly, so that only she could hear. Then he lowered his head and covered her lips with his.

CHAPTER FIVE

UNEXPECTED.

That was the only word she could come up with to describe the moment his mouth slid over hers. Oh, she'd wanted him to. Her heart had been screaming for him to do this ever since she'd curled into his side and let him pull her close.

She leaned her head a little further back so she could feel the full effect of his firm warm lips as they moved over hers.

A tiny sound exited her throat, and her mouth opened.

He hesitated. For a brief heart-stopping second he paused as if unsure whether to stop or continue.

Please, Jack. I just want this for a minute. Maybe two. Then I'll let you get back to your nice shiny life with your fancy football team.

I just need to know that someone, somewhere wants me.

Even if it's just for a moment.

His hand went from her neck to the back of her head, his fingers sliding deep into her hair as he remained poised over her mouth, lips just barely touching.

Then he did it. His tongue slid home with a smooth stroke that had her closing her eyes half in triumph, half in the heady luxury of the moment.

Norm wouldn't look back. He was used to giving his customers their privacy. And surely he'd had people make out in the back of his sleigh many times in the past. Not her, but generic people. She and Robert had certainly never done anything like this. She slid her hands beneath his coat, seeking the warmth between it and his shirt and debating whether or not she dared to duck beneath a second layer until she encountered bare skin.

Jack's fingers tightened in her hair, and he tugged her head back so their lips came apart. "What are you doing?"

Maybe he'd read her mind.

"I could ask you the same thing," she whispered. "What are you doing?"

"Right now, I'm wondering how long this ride is."

"At least an hour. But it can be as long as we want it to be."

Wow, had she really just said that? Evidently, because he gave a low groan that only she could hear and plastered his lips back to hers.

This time there was no question or hesitation, just a hard demand that she was more than happy to answer. Beneath the blanket, she worked his shirt free of his slacks until she had access to that smooth, firm skin she'd been thinking about. She allowed her fingers to slide to mid-abdomen.

Did he work out with the football players he took care of? Because there was some defined musculature beneath all these clothes. The sleigh turned another corner and her hand slipped further up, running over a hard masculine nipple.

Oops. She hadn't meant to do that, but now that she was here…

He moved from her mouth to her ear. "Don't."

Oh, but she already had. Her fingers circled again, testing, bumping and finally giving a little squeeze that had him hissing in a breath. "Mira."

And, oh, if she didn't love hearing her name muttered in that rough, sexy way.

Never had she gone out of her way to drive a man wild, but this one was different. He seemed so uptight. So...*unexpected.*

There was that word again.

Any other guy would have been happy to oblige by returning the favor. But not this one. He was acting like a stick of dynamite with a very short fuse.

He bit her earlobe once, twice, sending a desperate shiver over her. Deep down inside her, things were changing. Moistening. Transforming want into need at an alarming pace.

As if sensing the shift in her, he turned his body into hers, using his broad back to shield her from any prying eyes. Then one hand splayed low on her abdomen, taking her breath away as he held it there with firm pressure.

Yes. Please, Jack.

She wasn't sure what she was asking for—it

wasn't like they could just have sex in the back of Norm's sleigh. But she wanted something. Wanted to feel him in her hand, wanted to drive him over the edge into insanity. Even if she got nothing more out of it than that. She squeezed his nipple between her fingertips again to see if he felt the same way.

"You're playing with fire."

She blinked up at him. "Fire is the best known antidote to freezing temperatures, didn't you know?"

His hand skimmed up her hip and ducked beneath the hem of her shirt. His skin wasn't icy, like she'd expected, but yummy and warm with slight callusing on the pads of his fingers. He glanced back as if making sure their driver was still facing the front. "This is not a smart idea, you know."

"Never said it was." She squeezed again.

"Hell, woman." Just like that his hand swept up her side and cupped her breast, his thumb stroking across her bra-covered nipple and sending a shot of pure pleasure straight to her center.

Okay, maybe she hadn't been playing fair. But

neither was he, sitting beside her looking good enough to eat. And she was a little hungry. She could nibble, even if she couldn't get a full meal, right?

But the second she started to trail her fingers back down his stomach, she found her wrist gripped in a steel band. "No."

All playfulness was gone from his voice, and when she glanced at his face his eyes were dark, intense, a muscle working in his jaw. He slid his hand free of her shirt and tugged her clothing down. Pulled her coat back into place and buttoned it.

Her breath caught. Was he angry? Maybe she had carried this game a little too far. She started to withdraw, only to have his grip tighten, and he jerked her closer. His mouth moved back to her ear. "If we ever do this—and I'm not saying we will—it's not going to be some furtive little quickie, Mira. I want time, lots of it, and room to maneuver. Got it?"

She gulped. "Yes."

Whether she was acknowledging what he'd said or giving him permission she had no idea. But what else could she say? He'd taken her pass and intercepted it. The next play was with him.

With one last heart-stopping nip to her earlobe, he sat back and calmly straightened the blankets, while her pulse pounded madly in her ears.

"Now," he said as the first flakes of snow began falling again, "tell me about the local silver mines."

Jack wasn't sure where he'd gathered the willpower to stop her. It had been pretty obvious where she'd been headed once her hand had left his chest and traveled south. He could have let her continue…a few pumps and he'd have been done. Sated. But that's not what he wanted. If he was going to have her, he'd told the truth. He wanted hours. And he wanted to be able to use his hands. His mouth. He wanted to see her red hair spread out on a pillow and breathe in that purely feminine scent of her body.

Yes, he'd thought of having a fast encounter with some generic woman in his hotel room. But there was nothing generic about Mira. And he wasn't interested in a few brief seconds of pleasure.

Compared to what he really wanted from her, a hand job was like settling for a grilled cheese sandwich when what you craved was a sixteen-ounce rib eye.

She'd seemed a little glassy-eyed when he'd asked her about the mines, but he'd needed to get his own mind off of what he'd wanted to do and put it on something a little less explosive. Between that and the snow that had started to fall more freely he'd been able to cool his body down enough to keep from snatching her up and laying her down on that heated red velvet bench, driver or no driver.

By the end, she'd giggled as he'd reached into the pocket of his leather bomber and pulled out a beanie cap, pulling the black headwear down over her head to protect her from the white, powdery precipitation.

"I have my own, you know."

He couldn't resist a little shrug. "You look good in mine."

Once the ride was over, Mira thanked Norm

and gave him a quick hug before moving to Patsy and rubbing her thickly furred neck. "Thanks for that, you guys. It was great."

She promised to visit the stables more often, and the man tipped his hat and gave a courtly bow before climbing back on his sleigh and heading off again with another round of jingling bells and clip-clopping of hooves.

Then Jack—still in the throes of shaky reasoning and even shakier impulse control issues—had done the unthinkable. He'd asked Mira out again. Up on the slopes this time and ending with dinner in the restaurant.

And she'd done something just as unthinkable. She'd accepted.

"You have another date with him?" Ellory took a sip from her glass of Merlot and leaned a hip against the bar.

Mira squirmed. There was no way of avoiding it this time. Number Five might have become a problem. "Yes. But it's not like it's a big deal or anything. And the sleigh ride kind of got snowed out." But not before they'd done some necking in the back seat…and not before Jack had hinted he wanted to do darker things that involved time and lots of space.

She gulped a mouthful of her own wine.

How could she turn her back on something like that? Besides, it wasn't as if she was looking for a long-term relationship. This might even work in her favor. If they did have sex, she could prove to herself that she could have a one-night stand without it necessarily evolving into something permanent. Wasn't that what she was trying to avoid? Jack didn't live in the area. He'd soon be heading home to Texas. Back to his team.

No strings. No unexpected visits. No occasional sightings, like she had with her ex.

But did she want a one-night stand? Was she built that way?

If not, she'd better figure out how to change her personal blueprint because unless she never wanted to have sex again she was going to have to play by a new set of rules. One that involved a quick roll in the sheets and kicking the man in question out on the other side of the bed the next morning.

No regrets. No heart involvement.

It was the perfect solution, which was why she'd made that toast on New Year's Eve.

She glanced at her friend and took another—smaller—sip of her wine. "Don't worry, Elle, I'm sticking with the program. I'm not getting hung up on him. I'm following the spirit of the bet. You said that I wouldn't make it *past* Number Five. I never said I wouldn't go out with any of them more than once."

"Hmm…really? I understood that you would go out on a single date with twenty-five different men over the course of the year."

Mira tried to think back to the exact wording of that resolution. Had she said only one date apiece? She decided to play dumb. "So are you suddenly going to go all legalistic on me? The queen of all things loose and free?"

"*Touché.* You know me way too well." She sent Mira a grin and lifted her glass in salute before taking another drink of the dark red wine.

Relaxing onto one of the tall leather seats that surrounded the kidney-shaped bar, Mira swiveled around to face her friend. "Okay, so we'll say *intent*, then." She lifted her own glass. "Here's to intent. That I intend to steer clear of serious male-female relationships."

They clinked their glasses together. Ellory set her wine down on the polished wooden surface of the bar. "So let me get this straight. You're going to have no serious relationships with males or females? Well, that's a damn shame."

Mira swatted her arm. "Very funny. You know what I mean."

She laughed again. "Rats. Of course, I've sworn off men, too." She sighed. "So you're going to let man number five have another shot at getting this date thing right."

"Yep, although there's nothing to get right. We're just going to hit the slopes one more time tomorrow and get a bite to eat afterwards. Then it's done." Maybe. That was if she didn't fall into bed with the man right afterwards. A tingle of anticipation ran through her.

"Uh-oh. Speaking of hitting the slopes, ex-beau jerkwad at oh-three-hundred."

Mira blinked before she realized what her friend meant. She glanced to the right and saw

Robert nursing a beer far closer to them than she'd like. Their eyes met, and her ex lifted his glass to her. She just barely refrained from rolling her eyes. Was he worried she was going to run to Daddy and tattle about what he'd done? She should. Really she should, but she wanted nothing more to do with him. She was willing to let Robert save face to make that happen, although the creep didn't deserve it.

She turned away and met her friend's worried eyes.

"Did you take a good look at him?" Ellory asked.

"What?"

"Robert. I want you to memorize every last flaw that man has and imprint it on your memory." She leaned over and squeezed her hand. "Don't let someone do that to you again."

"I won't."

Ellory was right. She needed to use Robert as a cautionary tale and not toss away one bad apple only to immediately pick up a second one. Even if at least one part of that apple tasted as sweet as honey. Because who knew what she'd find when she turned it around and looked at the other side?

Although she suspected the back side of Number Five would look just as crisp and tasty as the front. And that was the biggest problem of all.

CHAPTER SIX

SHE WAS LATE.

Jack wasn't sure if he was happy about that or ticked. They'd agreed to ride up to the slopes together for another couple of lessons and then have dinner afterwards.

Propping his skis and poles against one of the heavy pillars that held up the wraparound porch, he inspected his snow boots for the fifth time. Yeah, yeah, yeah, all the laces were well tied and nothing dangled where it could trip him up. He'd leave that to the infuriating woman he'd almost mauled in the sleigh.

He hadn't been able to get her out of his head all weekend, which had seemed to drag. It had been made worse by a phone call from his coach making sure he was resting and having plenty of "fun."

As far as the resting went, it was hit and miss.

He'd slept fairly well one night, only to wake up in a cold sweat the next.

But was he having fun?

A little too much, if you asked him. He'd had no business letting things get so out of hand on that ride through the snow. His only excuse was the same pathetic one he'd given himself each time he'd been around the woman. It had been far too long since he'd gotten any.

And how crude did that sound? Paula would be so proud of what he'd become.

Except he remembered her having a little bit of naughty wrapped up in her nice. Maybe that's why Mira's outrageous behavior had bothered him so much. It struck too close to those memories he'd done his best to bury.

Bury. Not a good word to use. Since he'd literally buried the woman he'd loved since high school. The woman he'd gone through medical school with.

Maybe he should just do what he'd said and go to bed with Mira. Be done with it. Except she hadn't shown up yet, and she was now—he glanced at his watch—over a half-hour late. Even knowing she wasn't coming didn't stop him from waiting here like a pathetic loser, going over the thousand and one excuses she might have for standing him up.

None of them, except maybe her father becoming ill, held up. Especially since he'd just seen Mr. Dupris a few minutes earlier and had given him a half-wave as he'd strode through the entrance.

Well, nothing to do but go ahead on up and ski back down. He might as well get some use out of his rental fee. But somehow doing it alone held no appeal any more.

He grabbed his skis and poles and started toward the chairlifts that lay about fifty yards to his left.

"Jack, wait!"

A familiar voice sounded behind him. If he were smart, he'd just keep going and pretend he hadn't heard her. But, of course, he didn't. He turned around and all thoughts of leaving disappeared.

Mira, in the same all-white snow outfit she'd worn the other day, hurried toward him, equip-

ment slung over her left shoulder, her hair streaming around her shoulders. "Sorry. I thought you'd
be gone by now."

Thought...or hoped?

"Sorry to disappoint you." The words were
more difficult to force out than they should be.

She frowned, falling in step beside him. "Disappoint me? I had a patient this morning and
didn't have your cell number. I tried calling your
room, but you'd already left, evidently."

His cell number. It hadn't even dawned on him
to give it to her. And he had left early that morning, deciding to go for a walk in the crisp air to
clear his head and to try to talk himself out of
actually sleeping with the woman. When she
hadn't shown up, he'd thought she'd regretted
that terrible—or was it amazing?—kiss they'd
shared.

Now she was here. And he was just as torn over
what to do as ever.

Catching the next flight out of Silver Pass
would be the smart thing. But his coach would
probably not welcome him back with open arms

at this point. In fact, he might not welcome him back at all.

Maybe that wasn't such a bad thing, although what would he do with his life then? Allow it to spiral back down to dark places he'd rather not revisit? And if he sat around at home, that's exactly what would happen.

Regrets, he'd discovered, were a poison that didn't quite kill.

Two and a half more weeks.

He could always find Mrs. Botox and be done with it. He could guarantee there'd be no emotional entanglements on his part after spending a night with her.

So why did sleeping with Mira have to be any different?

It shouldn't, but he had a feeling it would be.

"Sorry about the cell number. I didn't even think to give it to you last night."

She grinned up at him. "I don't think either one of us was doing much thinking."

His own smile took him by surprise. "Probably not. How is your patient, by the way?"

"A child with an upset stomach. Judging from

the stack of crumbled candy wrappers on her nightstand, I think I found the culprit."

"Such an exciting practice you have here, Doctor."

She gave a slight grimace as they arrived at the chair lifts. "I'm sure it's not as action packed as yours, but it has its moments." She gestured at the line of running seats that swooped by before starting their ascent. "Do you know how to use one of these?"

"I've somehow gotten on them during both of my other outings, but I have to admit it wasn't pretty." He eyed the chairs. Mastering them certainly hadn't been as easy as it had looked. At least with surfing he simply lay on his board and paddled out from shore. Everything was done under his own power, which was how he preferred it.

She moved over to the bench and snapped her boots down onto her skis. "Put on your skis, and I'll talk you through the process."

Once they both had their skis situated, she had him stand and move over to the line with her, handing their passes to one of the attendants.

While various people got on the two-man lifts, she explained what they were doing. "We're next. Move to the mark."

He shuffled with her over to a blue line painted on the ground, and they waited for the couple ahead of them to sit on a chair and be carried up the mountain. Then they moved to the second line. "Look behind you," she said, "and keep the chair in sight. Once it gets to us, the attendant will hold it long enough for us to sit."

And just like that they were on, the lift swaying as it moved up over the snow. Mira snapped a protective bar down over them. He'd been so worried about his balance the last time he'd ridden up that he hadn't even realized the safety feature.

"Have you ever fallen off one of these?" he asked.

"Yes, as a child." She shifted her poles. "Did you fall the last time?"

"Off the ski-lift itself? No. But the first time I tried to move away from the chair? Yes." That had not been one of his better moments, and probably what had contributed to his fall down the slope itself little a while later. The one Mira had rescued him from.

The lift continued up the long ascent, and Jack tried to settle back and enjoy the view. It was beautiful, the range of white mountains stretching out, skiers looking much smaller than they actually were, even though the lift wasn't carrying them all that high.

But more than the view, or the worries about getting on or off the lift, was his concern about how aware he was of the woman next to him. Like the other times they'd skied, she was decked out all in white, but her helmet wasn't on her head yet, just the pink beanie she'd worn during their last outing on the slopes. The chair was small enough that their shoulders and arms touched, whether he wanted them to or not. And along with each bump or wobble came the memories of what they'd done in the sleigh. The way the motions of that vehicle had shifted them together until he hadn't been able to resist her.

This woman ramped him up, almost to the point of not caring who saw them. The truth was he hadn't wanted to stop during that ride, and he wasn't all that sure what had made him grab her hand just before she reached the belt on his slacks.

Maybe the realization that once she touched him there'd be no turning back. Or was it really as simple as what he'd said, that he wanted more time? More space?

Her fingers slid across the top of his hand, and he jerked his mind back from those chaotic thoughts to listen to what she was saying.

"There's the entrance to the silver mine I told you about." She pointed to something off in the distance about a half-mile away from the lodge. He could just make out brown wooden boards, but it appeared tiny from here. "It's closed to the public?" For some reason he thought maybe they'd made some of the mines into tourist attractions.

"Oh, yes. Not a safe place at all. There's a risk of avalanches out that way as well. We've had some snow, so the safety teams are monitoring the area. There are some off-piste skiing areas not far from there that could be affected."

"Off-what?"

"Off-piste. It means off the trail. Areas between the groomed runs. Some of them are open for skiing and some of them aren't. But here in Silver Pass those sections are reserved for advanced skiers, since there can be rocks and debris hidden beneath the snow—although we try to keep things marked well enough that people are aware of what's there."

"I don't think I'll be tackling any of those this trip."

"Chicken," she said with a smile. "We're almost at the end of the line." She nodded at the sign on the pole to the left that warned skiers to put the tips of their skis up.

Somehow, once they got to the offloading area, Jack managed to keep his skis pointed skyward and slide his ass off the chair, where he then glided down the little slope that led away from the circling chairs. And this time he didn't fall or careen into any other people who were exiting the lifts.

Grabbing onto a rope that was on the far side of the space, Mira slid smoothly beside him. "Good job!"

"Mira!" Her name came from across the way, and when she glanced over with a roll of her eyes he couldn't help but try to figure out who it was.

Ah, his former ski instructor and her ex. Standing at the top of the bunny slope, he was with a group of about twelve novice skiers. Even from here, though, he could sense the man's frown when Mira didn't answer him.

"You ready?" she said, her tight voice indicating she wanted to get away from there.

Judging from the steam he sensed gathering behind the other man's eyes, he nodded. "Why don't you go on? Unfortunately, I'm going to need to start with that beginner's hill again."

Mira gave him a cool glance. "Do you think I'm going to scamper off like a frightened rabbit?"

Hardly. He'd just thought she might want to avoid the guy.

They made their way over to the gentle slope, using poles and sidesteps until they were at the top. Although the instructor kept on teaching his charges how to slow their speed going down the hill, the man's eyes were obviously on them, probably wondering what the hell Jack was doing with her again.

Deciding to play by the other man's rules, Jack stared him down for a few seconds. Once the guy looked away and began to actively teach again, he noticed that Mira's attention wasn't on them but on the abandoned mine she'd pointed out from the ski lift. "What is it?" he asked.

"I don't know. Probably nothing." She gave a quick shrug then pulled one of her gloves off with her teeth before reaching in her pocket. She pulled out her phone and scrolled through something, glancing at the gray cloud cover a time or two. "Weird," she muttered, half to herself.

She put the phone in her pocket and then shoved her glove back on. "Do you want to lead or follow?"

"I always believe in letting ladies go first."

"Perfect. Because I like going first. That way, I can concentrate on getting to the good stuff."

Before he could decide if she was purposely being suggestive or not she'd used her poles to shove off the flat surface and start down the hill. He followed her, watching in awe as she expertly picked up speed and maneuvered from side to side. His balance felt pretty good today, but even so he couldn't match her speed, even using his poles to give himself some additional impetus from time to time. She was halfway to the bottom by the time he'd made it fifty yards.

Out of the corner of his eye he caught sight of another skier, coming just as fast as Mira had gone. Only this person sliced to the right just as he passed Jack, his skis sending out a large burst of snow that pelted him right in the chest. "Sorry about that, Number Five."

What the hell? Struggling not to lose his balance or his temper, he watched as the jerk proceeded on down the hill and did a quick zigzag as he came to Mira and then pulled in front of her, forcing her to come to a quick halt.

Jack frowned. That damn instructor again. He pushed his ski poles into the snow and forced himself to go faster, making sure his skis were aimed straight down the hill to speed his progress. By the time he reached her, though, the idiot had already left, heading toward the bottom in a series of moves geared to show off his skills to their best advantage. Well, that was all the man had going for him, from what Jack could tell.

"What was that all about?"

Mira's jaw was tight. "Nothing I can't handle."

"What is a number five? Is it some kind of ski-ers' code for 'make way' or something?"

"What?" Her face went very still.

"He skidded in the snow, hitting me with the stuff, then threw me an apology and said 'num-ber five'."

"I…" She took a deep breath and then tried again. "It doesn't mean anything."

Somehow he didn't believe her, because she hadn't given him a blank stare or said she had no idea what it meant. She'd said it didn't mean anything, as if she knew what the guy was talk-ing about but was discounting it.

She scooted closer and brushed some snow off his jacket. "Sorry he's such an ass."

What Jack couldn't understand was what Mira could have seen in a man like this. But he did like the way she'd sidled closer and the touch of her hands on his chest, even if there were ten tons of clothing between them.

"Did he get you too?"

"No. He was just trying to show off for his students."

It was more than that, but if she didn't want to get into it, who was he to try to force the issue?

She again pulled out her phone and glanced at it. "Do you mind if we head toward the mine? We won't go all the way or anything. There's another easy slope or two that we'll need to cover, but they're not much harder than this one. I just want to get a closer look at something."

"That's fine." The further away they got from her ex, the better Jack liked it. He wasn't worried about himself, he was pretty sure he could take the guy on solid, non-snow-covered ground, but he didn't want the bastard bothering Mira. "What do you want to look at?"

"I'm not sure. One of the snowdrifts looks a little iffy from here, but it could just be the angle. I'm not seeing any alerts on the weather site." She nodded at the sky. "But I think we might see another inch or two before the day's out."

Jack had noticed the thick cloud cover as well. He'd been glad for the shade, actually, as the sun glinted off the snow in a way that made his eyes burn, even with his goggles. "Will that be a problem for the resort?"

"It shouldn't be. I'll let you know when we get closer." She glanced back at him. "Follow me, okay, and don't go off the trails."

As if he would.

Slowly, Mira guided him down one slope, taking it slow and easy before sidestepping across a plateau and arriving at another well-groomed slope. No one seemed to take any notice of them, but Mira had checked her phone several more times. Jack had no idea what she was looking at, or even for.

A flick of ice hit his cheek and then another. He reached out to touch her jacket before they started down the next hill. "Do you feel that? I think the snow's started."

"That's what I was afraid of." She put her hand over her brow and seemed to scan the area.

Jack followed her line of sight, but all he saw were skiers going down various slopes, as well as another ski lift on the far side of the resort carrying people up the hills.

Jamming her poles into the snow, she scrolled through her phone, her finger sliding up the screen repeatedly as the occasional flake turned into a light snow shower. Then she bit her lip. "Jack, do you think you can make it back to the lodge on your own?"

"Why?" Was she texting her ex, getting ready to hook up with him or something?

No, she seemed genuinely worried about something.

"I'm not sure."

Jack heard a low rumble then it stopped. He cocked his head, listening. "Does it normally thunder during snowstorms?"

She didn't answer, just shoved her goggles on top of her head and jabbed her finger at her phone. Then she put it up to her ear. She waited and waited then someone evidently answered. She stared off into the distance. "It looks like some snow may have shifted over by the Vendry Mine." She waited and then continued. "No, I'm not positive, but I don't remember seeing it that far down on Friday evening."

Friday evening. When they'd been kissing in

the back of the sleigh? She'd paid attention to the snow cover by the mine? That's the last thing he'd been thinking about on that crazy ride. It stung his pride a bit that she'd been able to concentrate on things other than his mouth on hers.

She paused again. "And in case you haven't noticed, it's snowing again, and we got a couple of inches last night. I'd like you to let my dad know. He's not answering his cell." Her brows went up. "What do you mean, he went into town?"

Jack pulled his goggles up over his head as well when the snow kept hitting them and then melting, leaving behind droplets of water. Another roll of thunder came and went.

"I think you should call him and ask him to come back. I'm telling you, you need to be ready, just in case. Something's going on. Do you want me to have them clear the slopes?"

She waited for the other party to respond. "Are you sure?"

A puff of something that looked like a lazy roll of smoke sifted into the air over by the mine. A fire? There weren't many trees in that particular area, so he didn't think so. And Jack hadn't caught sight of any lightning, neither could he imagine anyone smoking while skiing.

"Okay. I'm going to stay up here for a while. I'll call you in a half-hour or so." She scrubbed her cheek against her shoulder. "Will do. Yeah, me too. Bye."

She hung up and scrolled again, then dropped the phone back into her pocket.

"Problem?" he asked, when her jaw remained tense. Had she been talking to the instructor?

As if realizing for the first time that he was still there, she slowly turned toward him. "Not really." She hesitated and then lifted her chin. "I don't want you to take this the wrong way, but maybe it would best if you headed back to the lodge."

Suspicion immediately flared in the back of his head. "Conversing with the ex?"

Why he'd said that, he wasn't sure. Even if she'd called him, it was pretty obvious it hadn't been to meet up with him or anything. She was worried about something over on that hill. Enough to want whoever was on the other end of that line to call her father and ask him to come back to the resort.

But his veiled accusation didn't go unnoticed. Her eyes chilled. "What I do or don't do is none of your business."

Okay, that had backfired. He'd hoped she'd give him a hint as to why she'd suddenly changed course, going from flirty to worried to angry in the space of a few minutes.

He touched her hand. "Sorry. I didn't mean it that way. I was digging for information, actually."

A thin layer of snow now covered the cute pink cap on her head and dotted her lashes. She smiled. "Okay, in case you're wondering—or even if you're not—I'm not going to get back together with my ex. Not now. Not ever. But I need to check something out, and I don't really want an inexperienced skier on any of those harder slopes."

"The ones closer to the mine."

She nodded. "The snow looks like it's moved, to me, shifted downward since our ride the other night."

"I heard you mention that, but what does it mean?"

"We got some snow last night. And we're due

for more tonight. Not a ton, but enough to add more weight to the already thick layer. If it slides any further there could be trouble."

He brushed a couple of flakes of snow off her nose with a gloved fingertip. Her cheeks were pink with cold, as was her nose, and she looked pretty damned adorable right now. In spite of her worried frown.

The thunder rolled again, and Mira immediately jerked around to the side and stared at the mine, where, sure enough, another puff of white erupted into the air. Not smoke. Snow. Just like when Mira's ex had sent a burst of it shooting toward him. Once disturbed, the finer stuff drifted into the air, while the heavier stuff had hit him and then fallen to the ski slope, where it had slipped downhill a few feet. Then it had rolled to a stop.

So if the puffs he saw over by the mine were snow vapor, then something was disturbing it. But what?

At that second the rumbling started up again, this time growing in volume. He vaguely heard Mira's "Oh, my God!" before what seemed like half the mountain began to move, sliding downward, giant plumes of vapor rising into the air. And below the action—on another set of slopes— was a group of about twenty skiers.

He finally understood what Mira was panicking about, his own chest tightening and his breathing shooting through the roof in response to what he was currently witnessing.

Because, like a tsunami that churned its way toward shore, an avalanche was slowly building up momentum. And it was headed right for that unsuspecting group.

CHAPTER SEVEN

"STAY HERE." MIRA'S only thought, once the rumbling stopped, was getting over to the site and helping get those people out.

One second skiers had been whizzing down the side of the mountain, and the next about seven people had been flattened by a crush of snow. The rest of the group had successfully outraced the front edge of the avalanche, joining those near the bottom of the slope who'd escaped unharmed. A few of them were trying to climb back up the steep hill to get to their companions. But who knew if or when the snow would shift again?

"I'm going with you."

"Jack, those slopes are very different from the one we're on now. I don't want to have to worry about you too."

"You won't have to." He motioned to the bottom of the hill. "I'll ski the rest of the way down and walk over. I've done some rock-climbing. I'll make my way back up. You can't handle that many injuries on your own."

He was right. Until help arrived, she was going to have her hands full.

"Okay, go."

He started down the hill, while Mira made the call to the office. They would already know about the avalanche, but she wanted to make sure they knew the numbers. When Chuck Miller answered, she was brief and to the point. "About seven skiers buried. Call in search and rescue. Tell them to get Anson Graves and his dog up here, just in case."

She'd worked with the search and rescue expert before. He was the best there was. She only hoped he could get here in time.

Pushing off with her poles, she began to quickly make her way across the slope in sweeping lateral motions—like a sailboat that had to go against the wind. She used the downward momentum to drive her to the side. The off-piste areas were more challenging, but Mira had been on the slopes all her life. They were nothing she hadn't done before. It wasn't normally under these kinds of circumstances, though.

One of her skis skated over a buried rock, and she lurched sideways before correcting herself, her heart loping across her chest for a few seconds. In the silence that followed the avalanche she could now hear muffled screams of those on the affected slope, as well as cries of dismay from other nearby skiers. Her ex caught up with her halfway to the site.

"What can I do?"

This wasn't the time for a war of words or anything else, and they both knew it. She needed as much help right now as she could get. "Gather up some of the other instructors and send them over to the slope. We have to see if we can get those people out, and fast." If the avalanche victims weren't rescued almost immediately, they'd die.

"On it." He didn't question her authority, just thumbed his phone and spoke to someone, before starting back down the slope with a quick salute.

Her glance went back to Jack. He was already at the bottom and had his skis off, leaving them where they were while he sprinted toward the other slope in his heavy boots.

Mira skied faster, taking a group of moguls in her stride as she stayed the course.

She glanced at her watch, keeping track of time as she knew oxygen deprivation caused by suffocation was a very real concern for avalanche victims, although the cold was one thing in their favor in that respect.

Two minutes. One more off-piste and she'd be there.

She took a deep breath as she ventured off the groomed slopes and onto the rugged terrain that separated her from her patients. This was one of the most challenging off-piste sections on the resort, and she'd only attempted it a couple of times. It was also one of the reasons she'd insisted that Jack not follow her across. She couldn't concentrate on getting to where she needed to be if she had to rescue Jack from a bad spill or crash.

She bypassed one tree, only to whizz past another so close that a branch caught at the sleeve of her jacket. She had to jerk her arm free to avoid being dragged sideways and off her feet. The sound of ripping fabric told her it had worked.

A few more yards of bumps and swerves as she made her way across, and then she came out of it, sailing onto the much smoother section to her left. The slope was steep and slick and it still took most of her concentration to navigate around unstable clumps of snow. Keeping her gaze focused on where she'd seen the small group of people go down, she sliced to a halt when her skis bogged down in a thicker drift. A few skiers had made it back up and were out of their skis, poking their poles into the snow. One person was digging about ten yards away.

"Found someone here," said the man closest to her.

Mira clicked out of her skis and slogged several yards in snow up to her thighs before dropping to her knees beside the man.

"Try to uncover the face first," she directed.

She immediately joined in scooping snow, hitting a jacket a few inches down. A black zipper ran down the middle of it. Thank God the person wasn't face down. They quickly worked their way up and found a young woman. Mira leaned down to feel her pulse and listen for signs of breathing.

There! A gasped breath and the flicker of eyelids.

"Can you stay here and uncover her as much as possible? Don't move her at all, though. I'm going to see if I can help some of the others."

Robert and Jack arrived within seconds of each other, and while Robert sent the other man an angry glare he didn't question his right to be there. He'd probably already heard that Jack was a doctor. And judging from the snide comment he'd lobbed at him on the way down the slope, her ex had overheard her and Ellory's conversation in the bar and knew about that stupid resolution of hers.

No time to worry about any of that right now. They had to get these people out of the snow. And fast. "Robert, I saw at least two others go down about twenty yards to your left."

"Right." Her ex headed toward to the spot.

"Help!" yelled someone to her right. "I found someone, but he's not breathing."

Suffocation and crush injuries were their biggest worries right now, although the last person she'd found had been closer to the surface than she'd expected.

Jack motioned to her. "I'll get it, you keep looking."

Waiting to make sure he successfully navigated to the location, she paused and her cellphone went off. She mashed the button. "Can't talk now."

"Anson's five minutes out." Chuck's voice came through.

"Got it."

She dumped her phone back into her jacket pocket while she fought her way through snow that was now almost hip deep as she joined in the search. No one that she'd seen had been much higher up on the slope than she was now, and even if they had been they'd have been knocked downhill some way from the force of the snow.

"Any idea how many are missing?" she yelled into the general melee. She'd counted seven, but it had been hard to tell how many had actually gone down.

"I don't know, but my brother is in here somewhere," a woman called back to her from ten yards down the hill.

Thank God this was a more advanced slope. She'd seen no children on it when that thing had come thundering down the mountain.

She pushed toward the woman, whose black tracks of mascara bore witness to her distress. "Where was he when you last saw him?"

"Right here." The woman pointed her pole in an arc.

"Okay, let's start there and work our way down, okay?" She came alongside the distraught woman. "Side by side." Glancing again at her watch, she saw that five minutes had now passed. Time was running out.

She turned her ski pole upside down so she didn't hurt whoever was down there.

Chop, chop, chop. She pushed the metal end into the ground repeatedly, hoping to hit something that was obviously not snow.

Chop, chop, chop.

In the background, she heard others as they shouted that they'd also found someone, but she couldn't worry about that right now. All of her father's ski instructors were certified in CPR, and they knew the drill about not moving anyone. Her biggest worry right now was finding everyone who was missing before they suffocated.

Chop, chop, thunk. There!

About two feet beneath the white surface, she'd hit something soft. "Here!"

The woman beside her immediately joined her in digging as fast as they could.

They uncovered a hand. Pale and still.

Move up. Hurry, Mira!

The angle of the arm told her the victim was pointed down the slope, but the snow had buoyed the back part of him up, so that his head was buried deeper than the rest of him. It seemed like forever before they'd dug down far enough to reach him. Hair. Hell. He was face down. Mira frantically scooped deeper, digging around his face, until she could reach beneath him.

No breath. She felt the side of his neck. No pulse.

She swore under her breath.

"We need to turn him over." And pray he didn't have a fracture along his spine or neck. If they couldn't get him breathing, that wasn't going to matter, though. He'd die.

It took an additional fifteen seconds before they'd uncovered enough of his body to try to shift him. He was a big guy. And heavy.

"Get on this side with me."

They both tried to lift him to turn him over, but there was so much snow packed tightly around him. Tears of frustration came to her eyes. Then Jack was there beside them.

She threw him a look of utter gratitude.

Getting between her and the victim's sister, he said, "Grab hold of whatever you can on his far side. We need to pull him up sideways first, in order to flip him. There's not enough room to turn him where he is. On three."

"One, two…*three*!" They all pulled as hard as they could. The man budged, started to turn, and then Mira slipped, losing her grip on the man's jacket. She swore, louder this time.

"Again," she said.

Robert evidently saw their struggles, because he came up beside her. "Anson's just gotten here. Let me help."

He urged the man's sister to move so he could take her place.

Jack didn't even spare her ex a glance. "On three."

This time, when he hit three, they pulled and the victim flipped onto his side as the trio used the momentum to haul him up out of the hole.

Mira glanced over the surface of the snow long enough to see that Anson and his dog were indeed on the scene, the rescue animal already with his nose to the snow.

Jack did what she'd done a moment ago and checked for a pulse. "Nothing. You start chest compressions."

In the background, the man's sister started crying.

"Robert."

That was all she needed to say. Her ex moved toward the woman to keep her back, while she and Jack worked. She ripped open the guy's jacket, no longer worried about hypothermia or anything that didn't relate to his heart or lungs.

Quickly finding the sweet spot on his chest, she lapped one hand over the other, her palms thrusting downward in quick bursts as she counted aloud. His body sank in the snow a few inches from the force of her compressions, but the weight helped pack it down to form a solid enough surface to do some good. "One, two, three…"

No liquid came out of the man's lungs as she continued compressions, so his airway wasn't blocked by melted snow. Jack had evidently known to wait a few seconds to make sure of that fact, because by the fifth beat he'd tilted the man's head back and leaned over him to give mouth-to-mouth between her measured pulses. He lifted his head long enough to say, "Tell me when you need me to spell you."

She couldn't think about that or anything else right now, except what she was doing. With each push of her joined palms she chanted, "Breathe, breathe, breathe," willing the victim to fight. To live.

About a minute later she heard the most beautiful sound in the world. A gasp. Then a cough. Mira stopped what she was doing and reached for his neck, only to find that Jack's fingers were already there. Icy cold without his gloves, but real and alive. Just like their victim, whose eyes now moved beneath his eyelids.

Mira glanced at Jack. Without his quick thinking they might still have been trying to figure out how to turn the man in that hole. A few minutes longer and this scene might have ended very differently.

Jack's gaze met hers, and he gave a quick nod of triumph. She couldn't hold back her smile or her mouthed, "Thank you."

Her fingers were still over his, and he turned his hand and captured them, giving a quick squeeze. The backs of her eyelids prickled, before she forced herself to pull back. Robert still stood over them, his arm around the victim's sister.

"Thanks," she said to her ex. "Can you go find out who else needs help? Check with Anson and see what he wants us to do."

Robert's jaw tightened, and he eyed her for a second before giving a stiff nod and moving away.

Motioning to the woman, who was staring down, both hands over her mouth, Mira said, "He's breathing. Why don't you sit next to him and talk to him while we check him for other injuries?"

The woman dropped to her knees, her hands reaching into the depression in the snow and cupping her brother's cheeks. "Marty, I'm right here."

The man's eyes finally opened, focusing on the woman. He tried to say something but his sister stopped him, tears streaming down her face. "Let them make sure you're okay."

Mira worked on one side of the victim while Jack stayed on the other. No obvious broken bones, and by the way the man's limbs were starting to move around, his spinal cord was intact. Thank God, after the way they'd had to haul him up. They still had to be careful, though. Just because he could move it didn't mean he was out of the woods.

"Your other resus? Did you get him breathing?"

"Yes." He glanced at her. "They've accounted for everyone we know of. All doing okay."

Mira lifted her head so she could look over the snow. The woman she'd dug up at the beginning was now on her feet, someone braced beneath one arm as they watched the rest of the rescues. Anson and his dog were further to the right, far away from the rest of them. Could someone have been carried that far away?

It was as if Jack had heard her thoughts. "It reminds me of an undertow. It just drags you down and carries you with it."

She nodded. She'd never been around the ocean very much but she could see how the two might be similar in nature. Whether you suffocated in the snow or drowned, it was the same death. The same terror.

The man beneath them began struggling in earnest. "You need to lie still. You might have injuries we can't see."

His sister shushed him and gave him a fierce frown. Whether he was just exhausted or had realized what he was doing, he did as they asked.

"Can you zip his jacket back up?" Mira asked. "I don't want him to get any colder than he already is."

EMS arrived on the scene—several squads of men from the looks of it—swarming toward them, stretchers either in tow or folded into packs that were strapped to their backs. It was slow going, though, because this section of the ski resort boasted steep inclines geared toward the most experienced of their guests. But the rescue workers were prepared, the snow cleats attached to their boots grabbing at the surface, whether snowy or slick, with each step they took.

Jack climbed to his feet and made his way over to one of the workers, probably giving him an abbreviated version of what had happened.

A moment later a megaphone sounded through the group. "If you're with an avalanche victim, please raise your hand, and one of us will make our way to you."

Seven hands went up in all, including hers. Everyone was alive, from what she could tell.

Mira glanced anxiously at Anson to see if they were having any luck. She'd assumed there were only seven victims. Had she missed one somehow?

One of the emergency workers reached her. She recognized him. "Hi, Mike. Thanks."

"No problem. What've you got?"

She quickly went through the rescue and then

helped get a fresh set of vitals and stabilize the patient's neck. Mike took the pack off his back and unfolded it into a kind of stretcher-sled combo that could be eased down the hill.

Jack helped with another victim, while a handful of ski instructors helped with some of the others.

From around a hundred yards away Anson's dog gave a quick set of plaintive barks that sent a shiver through her. He'd found someone. She glanced down at her watch then closed her eyes and said a short prayer. Twenty minutes.

It had seemed like no time at all, they'd all been working so hard, and yet for whoever was buried it had been an eternity.

Jack reached Anson first and they went to work, shoveling snow. Mira cleared her current patient and got to her feet, giving the victim's sister a quick smile of encouragement to hide her own anxious heart. She made her way toward the pair, who'd now stopped digging. They'd located whoever it was.

Jack hopped down into the depression in the snow and did some quick maneuvering before his head disappeared as he knelt. In less than a minute he climbed back out again. Even from there she could see his tight jaw. The way he shook his head at Anson.

Oh, no!

She stopped where she was, her eyes shutting for a second or two. Then she wrenched her lids apart. There was still time. The snow could slow body processes down for a while. Jack knew nothing about the mountains, he could assume things that weren't necessarily true.

Surely Anson wouldn't give up that easily. Anger unfurled within her and she moved quicker, her boots slipping a time or two as she tried to run through the drifts.

They were wasting time!

When she reached the pair, she snarled at them, "Help me get the victim up."

"It's too late." Jack grabbed her arm.

"It's not. The snow sometimes lowers the body temperature so that…" She glanced down at the victim and her words caught in her throat.

Snow-clouded eyes stared up at them from

about three feet beneath the surface. And his neck…

She swallowed. Jack was right. There was nothing they could do.

The dog whined a time or two and pawed at the snow as if he didn't understand what they were waiting for. Anson dropped a hand onto the animal's head and gave him a quick scratch behind the ears, although when his eyes met hers they were grim. How often had the rescuer gone in search of a live person and come back with a body instead?

"Damn." She scrubbed her palms over her cheeks, surprised to find them moist and cold. "Let's get the others out first." She lowered her voice. "No one has mentioned not finding someone, and by now everyone at the resort must know about the avalanche. He's either here alone or someone's waiting back in one of the guest rooms. We'll need to see if he has some ID."

Jack came over to stand beside her. "Even if we'd found him sooner, it wouldn't have changed anything. You know that, right?" He put an arm around her and squeezed her shoulders. "There wasn't enough time to clear the slopes before it hit, even if we'd started across right after you noticed the first movement."

"I know." She couldn't stop herself from leaning a little closer, and then glanced over at Anson. "Thank you for coming."

"Any possibility that anyone else could be under here?"

"I tried to keep count as the avalanche came down. I thought there were only seven people buried, but…" she motioned toward the victim "…this makes eight."

Anson nodded. "I'll go ask at the lobby to see if anyone is missing and then do one more sweep of the area." He paused. "I don't want to leave until we're sure everyone is out."

"Agreed," Mira said. "While you're at it, can you ask Security to start contacting the guests to make sure everyone is accounted for? My dad should be back by now."

"No problem."

"Thanks again."

As she watched Anson and his dog head down

the slope, a shudder swept through her body. She was freezing cold, even with all her gear on.

Jack pulled her closer and eased her several yards to the right, away from the poor avalanche victim. Most of the other patients had either been transported or were in the process of being loaded onto stretchers. "You need to get back to the lodge."

"Not before everyone is out. It's part of my job—and it's the right thing to do." She straightened. "But you go ahead. Thanks. You're not having much of a vacation, are you?"

"That's okay. Wasn't my idea to take a vacation in the first place."

He'd mentioned that before. Who came to a ski resort against their will?

A horrible thought came to her. "Are you married?"

He pulled back, dropping his arm from her shoulders and meeting her eyes with a frown. "Are you serious? Have you forgotten that sleigh ride?"

She swallowed. No. Not for a second. "That doesn't always mean anything." Who knew that better than she did? Her dad hadn't respected his vows, and neither had her ex. She and Robert might not have been married but they'd been heading that way.

"It might not mean anything up here, but it does where I come from."

"Meaning?"

"Evidently people up here on the slopes play loose and easy with their marriage vows."

And how did he know…? Oh! Mrs. Botox.

"Those kinds of people live all over the world. Even in Texas."

"Well, I'm not one of them." His eyes, dark with some intense emotion, stared right through her for a second before he took a deep breath. "Sorry. That was uncalled for."

Yes, it had been. But she could see how he might have taken her words. "It's okay." Another shiver went through her. Her hands went into her pocket to find her gloves, only to remember that she'd ripped them off to do chest compressions earlier. They were still over on the other side of the slope.

She turned, thinking she was going to retrieve

them, when Jack pulled his out of his pocket. "Put these on."

"Oh, but—"

"Do it." He touched his fingers to hers. "I'm not as cold as you are."

It was true. His hands weren't warm, by any stretch of the imagination, but next to her stiff fingers his were like a tropical paradise.

One she didn't dare think about right now.

"Okay." She slipped her hands into the thickly lined fingers, smiling when Jack pulled her hat further down over her ears. "Thanks."

"No problem." He smiled back at her. "Lady, I have to tell you, you have a strange idea of a date."

"I wouldn't exactly call this a date." It may have started out that way, but it certainly hadn't ended the way she'd envisioned.

"Neither would I." His thumb slid along her cheek. "It's one thing after another when you're around."

"Believe me, I'd rather there were no such things as avalanches." Her eyes went to the shovel sticking up out of the snow near the last victim.

The whole lodge would mourn the man as if he were one of their own. These guests, even though they knew the risks of winter sports, never expected it to happen to them. And as careful as her father was, Mother Nature could—and sometimes did—trample right over the resort's precautions. "I hate that this happened."

"I know." His arm went back around her.

It felt good. Comforting. She was used to being the only doctor around this place. It was nice to have someone to share this particular burden with. And she honestly wasn't sure she could have handled this on her own. The worst thing she'd encountered other than the odd ski injury had been a norovirus outbreak that had swept through the ski resort three years ago, making a third of the guests and staff sick before they'd finally been able to contain it.

"Thank you for your help."

"I'm glad I was here."

"Even if being here wasn't your idea?" She couldn't help tossing his earlier words back at him.

He was tugging her further away from the site

when two rescue workers arrived with a basket and some more digging equipment.

Now that most of the patients had been cleared from the area, the other skiers had also headed down, no doubt urged by the ski instructors to clear this part of the mountain until further notice.

Anson came by and gave her a half-wave and said her dad and some others were working on contacting the rest of the guests. He was fairly confident no one else was under the snow, so he was headed back to the station to check in and fill out a report.

As soon as he was gone, Jack turned to her. "It might not have been my idea to come but I'm beginning to think my coach might have known what he was talking about."

"And what was that?"

He hesitated, then finally said, "Long story."

"Fair enough." He didn't owe her any explanations. He was simply man number five. It was better if she didn't know anything about him— well, except for the marriage thing. She'd have to remind herself to verify the marital status of any other man she went out with. She'd looked for the obvious thing, like a ring, but hadn't bothered doing that with anyone else.

Then again, she hadn't expected to go out multiple times with the same man.

She frowned. Now was probably as good a time as any to make her escape and move forward, otherwise she would just end up in the same old rut. Attracted to a man who wasn't what she needed him to be. He'd said it himself. He hadn't wanted to come. Preferred the surf to the snow.

Definitely not compatible. If she hadn't been able to make it work with a man—make that *three* men—who were from the Silver Pass area, why would she even think about getting attached to someone who not only wasn't from here but had no interest in sticking around?

Before she could say anything, though, he reached over and gripped her hand. "Walk you down?"

"Thanks. I'd like that."

Okay, so she could put off this whole separation process until she got back to her room. She wasn't even going to worry about dinner. Then, with their date officially over, she could sleep knowing this little bump in the road had been successfully navigated. She could tell Ellory she was moving on.

Life would continue, and Jack—no matter how tempting it might be to linger for a while and let him throw that rare smile her way—would be in her rear-view mirror, his reflection growing smaller and smaller with each day that passed. Until, finally, he was gone. Back to his home team. Back to his life with his coach and his friends.

And out of her life, forever.

CHAPTER EIGHT

MIRA HAD DESERTED HIM.

With dinner behind them and the night closing in fast, Jack sat at the bar, wondering exactly how he'd gotten here. After the shock of the avalanche and subsequent rescue efforts had worn off, it would have been easy to just cancel their plans to eat at the restaurant and go back to their rooms. Alone.

And yet once they'd come off that slope and stood in the arched doorway of the lodge, the words had come out of his mouth of their own volition. "Are we still on for dinner?"

She hadn't paused, even for a second, before saying yes.

Jack wasn't sure why he wanted it so badly, but he did. Maybe he wasn't quite ready to be by himself. Seeing that person's death earlier today had shaken him. Would someone grieve for the victim the way he'd grieved for Paula?

He ordered his first drink of the trip—other than that spiked hot chocolate—from the bartender and took a healthy swallow.

His wife had helped so many people. Worked tirelessly for her young patients, even when hope had seemingly been lost, to make sure they'd been cared for and comfortable all the way to the end. And he'd taken that away from her—had taken it away from those she could have helped in the future. She had been brilliant in her field. One of the best. And now she was gone.

All because he'd wanted to play doctor with a damn sports team. Lining up their specialties side by side, he'd known which one gave more value to mankind. But none of that had mattered at the time. Because he'd wanted that job. Had wanted it badly. And now none of it meant anything.

He'd seen that same special spark that Paula had possessed in Mira today. She'd been up on that mountain when the avalanche had hit. No one had known if that snow was going to shift again or not. She could have simply called in the

rescue teams and waited for them to get the sur-
vivors out before she'd begun treatment.

But she hadn't. She'd been one of the first on
the scene, digging right alongside the relatives
and friends of the victims. And the way she'd
run toward him and that rescue worker, fire in
her eyes as she'd yelled at them to pull the last
man out of the snow, saying there was still hope.

Something his wife had said constantly. *There's
always hope.*

Until, of course, there wasn't. Until a plane—
a plane Jack had asked her to be on—had gone
down in a ball of fire. Until hope had been
snuffed out by reality.

Just like in Mira's eyes when she'd looked into
that hole in the snow and seen the truth. That
there had been no hope.

His brain headed down familiar dark paths. He
took another sip of his drink. Relished the steady
burn of the alcohol as it trickled down his throat
and hit his gut.

Dinner had been good, helping him relax and
forget all the reasons he should be avoiding Mira
like the plague. She'd made him smile time and

time again, her animated expressions changing with each subject. She was passionate and beautiful, and he'd decided he could watch her talk all evening.

Only now she was on the other side of the room, talking just as passionately to her friend, the blonde.

Ellory, wasn't it?

An argument? No, he didn't think so. It looked more like Mira was trying to get the other woman to agree with her, palms facing up, their faces close together. In fact, it resembled some of the huddles he'd seen during games, when players had planned their next move.

Except this was hardly a play on a football field.

Break! A quick hug and a smile and then they were done.

Sometime during dinner, as he'd watched her laugh, he'd had some very bad thoughts. He'd entertained them all the way up to the last few minutes when guilt had wormed its way through him, devouring everything in its path. It happened every time he let his guard down.

Mira glanced his way and her shoulders went back, as if she'd come to some kind of decision.

What the hell?

As quickly as she'd left she was back, standing in front of him, hands on her hips, eyes on his face.

"What?" he asked, setting his glass on the bar.

"Nothing." She stopped for a second and cleared her throat. "Just seeing if I can get up the nerve."

"The nerve to…?"

"Ask you if you want to get out of here."

The words were so unexpected they shoved the breath from his chest. He sat on his barstool like a lump for several seconds. Had he just walked into an alternate universe? One where his wildest imaginings suddenly became reality?

Whatever universe it was, his body decided it much preferred this one to the one he'd just been in, reacting to the innuendo with a slow unfurling of a certain flag.

He decided to make sure he wasn't mistaken before he let his thoughts run any further ahead.

"Get out of here and go where?"

"Your room. My room. Take your pick." She looked closer at his face, her brows puckering. "Unless you don't want to."

Nothing plainer than that. In fact, the man sitting on the next barstool looked at her so quickly that his head nearly flew off his neck. And the expression on his face? *Hey, buddy, if you're not going to take her up on it, then clear out.*

Like hell!

"My room." Better stick to his own territory. Only…

Damn. He hadn't brought anything with him. This whole vacation had been taken under duress, he certainly hadn't expected to have a woman invite him back to her room.

The guy on the barstool was still ogling Mira from behind. Jack sent him a scowl that told him to back off in no uncertain terms. Then he threw some bills onto the bar, got off his seat, and grabbed Mira by the hand. In the distance, her friend watched them.

So what?

He got as far as the hallway and then glanced down the length of the space to make sure they were alone. Then he moved in. Close. Chest to her breasts with just enough pressure to send a jolt of desire arcing through his gut.

His cheek slid along hers, scooping up her scent—vanilla and snow—and absorbing the soft feel of her skin. He journeyed toward her ear. Arrived.

"Now, see, Mira, you have me at a disadvantage. I want nothing more than to drag you back to my room, but unless your gift shop carries… certain items…"

"I have no idea, but it doesn't matter." Her head went back, and she stared at him for a second. "Ellory thinks I need to sleep with you. Get whatever…" she motioned between the two of them "…this is out of my system."

Ellory. The friend.

So he wasn't the only one who'd felt the sparks. Who'd experienced the chemical heat that sizzled any time they were together. "So, am I 'in' your system?"

"Definitely. She thinks it's why I can't move…" She shook her head. "I don't normally do flings, but I think I want to make an exception in your case. So if you're clean, I'm on the Pill."

On the Pill.

Because she'd been sleeping with that oaf of a ski instructor?

Not fair, Jack.

Another thought came to him. "Are you trying to make your ex jealous?"

He couldn't say for a certainty he would refuse to go with her, even if that were the case. He'd wanted this woman ever since she'd stood over him in the snow and offered him her hand.

Why? Why now?

He had no idea, unless it was because he was out of his comfort zone—away from his team. Maybe he was just tired of wallowing in a vat of grief and self-pity. Paula would be horrified to see what he'd become.

Mira shook her head. "My ex will remain my ex for evermore. But if you're trying to get me out of the mood, it's working."

She started to slide out from beneath his body, and instinct had his hands going to the wall on either side of her, caging her in. "Sorry. Yes, I'm clean. And if you're looking for a fling, I'm your man." His lips found her jaw and skated along it. "I have to warn you, though. I wasn't expecting company, so my room might be a mess."

Tilting her head back as he made his way down the side of her neck, she murmured. "If you think I'm interested in looking at your…room, you're very much mistaken."

Part of his anatomy went haywire at the image of her reclining on his bed looking him over and putting her own special seal of approval on him. "I think I can find other things to occupy your thoughts."

She relaxed. "Think so?"

"Pretty sure."

He forced himself to stand upright, although all he wanted to do was take her mouth and make it his. But he could wait. He *would* wait.

Wrapping his fingers around her hand again, he started down the hallway toward the elevators. "Do you have to check on any of those patients from the avalanche?"

"They've all been taken to the hospital. The

staff has my cell number, if they need to get in touch with me."

He got into the elevator and punched the button for the top floor. Mira's eyes widened. "You're in one of the penthouse suites?"

"My coach, remember? I didn't book the room."

She leaned against the wall. "Your coach has good taste. And a hefty bankroll."

He snagged her hips and dragged her against him. "They spared no expense."

"They must like you an awful lot," she murmured, looping her arms around his neck.

The last thing he wanted to do was talk about his coach, or how much they were or weren't willing to fork out to get him back up to snuff. "And what about you? Do you like me?"

A shadow went through her eyes before it was gone. "I wouldn't have asked you if I didn't."

At least they both knew where the other stood. Jack didn't have to worry about Mira getting hung up on him or deciding she wanted to take things to the next level, because he couldn't. Not now. Probably not ever. She wanted a fling. And he'd been thinking that it had been too long since he'd been with a woman. They were both on the same page. And after tonight they could turn that page and never revisit it.

Mira waited outside the door as Jack slid his key-card into the lock and listened for the familiar snick as it released. She'd been in these rooms before, of course, but never as a guest. She'd for-gotten that pro football players made millions of dollars a year. But even if she'd remembered, she wouldn't have expected Jack to make as much.

Besides, after her talk with Ellory—where Mira had grilled her about whether or not she'd told Robert about their bet—she'd wondered if her friend was right. Whether a naughty romp with the man in question would solve her problems once and for all—or if that was a plan doomed to fail. She was attracted to Jack. Very attracted. Which is why she couldn't quite move on to the next guy.

So, Ellory's answer? Sleep with the man. Kind of a wash-that-man-right-out-of-your-hair move that would clear him from her system. It had worked for Ellory in the past, so it should be just as easy for her.

Jack pushed the door open, and she stepped into the large marble foyer. While the downstairs portion of the lodge was a study in rustic furnishings, this room went in the other direction, its sleek, modern touches hinting at wealth rather than shouting it from the rooftops. From the white plush carpet to the glimmering stainless-steel accents, the room reflected the snowy setting outside.

He shoved the door shut with his foot. "I thought you weren't interested in my room." The words had a smile behind them, but she jerked around to look at him anyway.

"I'd forgotten how nice the penthouse suites were." Where was that mess he'd mentioned? The room seemed as clean as a whistle.

He glanced around. "They are nice." Motioning toward the tiled wet bar on the other side of the living room, he asked, "Do you want a drink?"

Yes. She did. And now that she was here she was beginning to wonder what she was thinking. She couldn't believe she'd actually propositioned the man, something she'd never done in her life. But she hadn't been able to think of a way to casually head him in this direction, and she had no desire to hang around the bar, hoping he'd make a move. So she'd decided to pull an Ellory and take the bull by the horns.

And now that she had him? What exactly did she do with him? Tell him to strip naked and get to work?

A drink. She'd start with that. "I'd love one. Red wine, if there's one of those mini-bottles somewhere around."

"I'm afraid this room doesn't have a mini-anything. It's all big."

He was right on that front. Her eyes went to the man as he walked toward the bar. The room was huge, but Jack's height and frame made it seem almost ordinary. And that butt she'd admired a week ago...

She swallowed, changing her mind about the wine. "Jack?"

"Mmm?" He walked behind the bar and retrieved two glasses from a stand beside the sink.

"Would you mind if I skipped the drink?" She

twisted her hands in front of her, wishing she was better at this whole seduction gig.

He set the glasses down, and brown eyes bored into hers. "I was just thinking the same thing." He leaned his elbows on the polished wood surface. "Come here."

On legs that were suddenly shaking she made her way toward him, until she was on the other side of the counter. He crooked his finger. "Closer."

She licked her lips then leaned over the surface until she was within inches of him.

"Nice." One of his hands came up to cup the nape of her neck, fingers threading through her hair. He tugged her nearer until they were mouth to mouth. "Is this more along the lines of what you were thinking?"

"Yes," she whispered.

"Good." His mouth met hers with a sweet pressure that made her want to melt against him, made her wonder if she could leap across the barrier and grab handfuls of his shirt and haul him against her. But she didn't act on any of those thoughts. She stood there, leaning as close as she could get while his lips slid over hers time and time again. His teeth played with her lower lip, teasing it, until all she wanted was him hard against them, thrusting into her mouth like he'd done on the sleigh ride. Only tonight there was no Norm or Patsy to catch them in the act. It was just her and Jack. And this time she had no intention of stopping.

Her hands went up and caught his head when he started to move away from her mouth.

Uh-uh. That hadn't been nearly enough. She wanted him right there.

She eased him back to her mouth, and this time she opened, hoping to tempt him into sticking around for a while. With a low sound his hand tightened in her hair and the kiss morphed into something else. Harder. More demanding. His tongue pushed past her lips with a quick thrust that made her gasp. He filled her, head turning sideways so he could reach even deeper.

A moan worked its way up from inside her as he released the pressure, only to surge forward again. When he finally lifted his head she dragged in deep breaths, trying to clear her fuzzy brain.

"You're still too far away," he murmured. Taking her hand, he led her around the bar until she was at the spot he'd been standing seconds earlier. "Better."

He proceeded to drug her with several long, wet kisses that had her insides quivering with need. His hands slid down her sides, until he came to her waist, which he gripped. "When I say three, jump."

Her breathing still erratic, she somehow managed to spring up when he hit the number, finding herself perched on the glossy wood bar, looking down at him. When she frowned, wondering what he was doing, he backed up with a smile and then yanked his dark shirt up and over his head.

Ooh, she liked that. Her glance skated over his bare torso. Strong and muscular without being bulky, his tanned skin had obviously been kissed many times by the sun.

Surfer dude...football doc. That's right.

A smattering of dark hair started at his chest

and flowed downward, narrowing until it was just a slim, fascinating line that disappeared beneath the waistband of snug black jeans. When her eyes finally came back up, she found him watching her. Her teeth gnawed her bottom lip when he came forward, his warm palms landing on her thighs just above her knees and slowly smoothing along the surface of her legs. Her mouth went dry the higher he got, his thumbs grazing the sensitive area just inside her thighs.

Oh, man.

Then his hands were on her hips, and he jerked her forward until she was balanced on the very edge of the high bar, her thighs parting on either side of his chest. She felt open and exposed and the slow smile he gave her said that's exactly how he wanted her.

"Remind me to thank whoever put this bar in my room."

Since that was probably her dad, there was no way she was reminding him of anything.

He moved deeper between her legs and leaned over to plant a kiss on her stomach, sliding his hands beneath her shirt and pushing it up, until his lips grazed bare skin rather than her white tee shirt. His tongue dragged up her stomach, her muscles rippling in the wake of his touch.

Almost against her will, her eyes fluttered closed and her fingers went to his shoulders as he continued to kiss his way across her belly. When he reached the hip that lay just above the top edge of her jeans, he nipped at the bone, sending a quiver of electricity arcing right down to the parting of her legs. She ached for some type of pressure, but there was only air between her and his chest with no way of inching any closer. Not unless she wanted to fall off the bar. And there was no way she wanted to distract him from his current task.

His fingers went to the button on her jeans and had it open within a second, the zipper following soon afterwards. For once she was glad she'd put on feminine lacy panties and not her utilitarian black cotton undies.

As if reading her thoughts, his growled "Nice" hit her ears, making her smile.

The smile disappeared when he looked up the

length of her body. "I'm going to need your help for a second. You lift, and I'll slide."

Why that raised a decadent picture, she had no idea, but the image of her hips coming up while he slid home swamped her brain, making it difficult to obey his command.

Lift. He said lift.

Bracing her hands on either side of her hips, she lifted up while Jack tugged her jeans down her thighs and then her legs as she returned to her seated position.

His fingers trailed around the top band of elastic on her panties and slid under the lace ties at the sides. "I am going to enjoy undoing these. But first let's take care of that shirt."

He stepped back, making her frown.

What?

Wasn't he going to help her with that as well? When his arms went over his chest she had her answer.

It was either put up or shut up. And she was definitely aiming for the "put up" side of the equation. As in…grabbing the bottom of her shirt, raising her arms and dragging it over her head. She then let it drop onto the floor behind the bar.

Her bra matched her panties, both peek-a-boo pieces of lingerie that did a whole lot more peeking than anything else. She found her courage from somewhere. "Bra?"

"Not yet." Stepping forward again, he planted his hands on her knees and slowly pushed them apart until he was back between them.

Too late, she realized what he was planning when his lips pressed against the skin of her rib cage, just below her bra, and moved on a slowly winding path that headed south. He reached her belly button, dipping inside for a second, then the tip of his tongue toyed with the upper edge of her panties.

"Jack."

Plea? Or protest?

She wasn't sure. Only knew that he'd finagled things so she couldn't clamp her legs closed, and all the parts that mattered were well aware of that fact, pulsing with a heavy need she hadn't felt in a very long time.

His fingers came up and found the ends of the

ties on either side of her underwear. "Do you want me to stop?"

If she said yes, it would be all over. He hadn't said it, but she knew herself well enough to know it was true. She'd be too embarrassed to continue. And in truth she didn't want him to quit. Wanted him to show her exactly what he wanted from her.

And she had a feeling she wouldn't be sorry.

"No. Please, don't stop."

His eyes closed for a beat or two, hiding those gorgeous brown irises. Then they opened back up. "I'm going to make you say those words again in a very short while."

She gulped as a wave of awareness swamped her just as he tugged those ties and released the knots. Her underwear fell away, the front and back panels dropping to the bar. Jack wrapped his arms around her butt and pulled her hard against his chest, until that center part connected with his bare skin.

"Ah." She wanted nothing more than to grind against him in a frenzy but, as suddenly as he'd made contact, he pulled away again, the cool air flowing against her and making her squirm with need.

Lord. What was he doing to her?

"Take me to the bedroom." She was more than ready to have him right there, inside her, giving her the relief her body was starving for.

He kissed her stomach. "Soon." The warmth of his breath rolled across her skin. "Do you remember what I said up on that mountain?"

He wanted her to remember…*words*? At a time like this? With the heat his body was putting out? "No."

His hands were back at the tops of her thighs, thumbs pressing just enough to let her know he was there. "That's a shame. Because this would be such a great demonstration of that gentleman's rule."

Ladies first. That's what he'd said.

As his lips lowered to the top of her right thigh and kissed it, a shudder rolled across her. "That's not necessary. Let's just go to bed. I—I want to."

"Oh, sweetheart. So do I. More than you can possibly know." He kissed the inner surface, teeth nipping at the tender flesh. "But I can't. Not yet."

He pushed her legs wider as his lips ventured closer to a very dangerous area. "Intoxicating. Your scent. The taste of your skin." The words muttered against her sent fire rushing through her veins and anticipation clenching through her stomach. Then he was there, and the shock of his tongue making gentle inroads made her go completely still. She had to prop herself up on her elbows to keep from falling backwards at the rush of sensation as he slid up and around, avoiding that one tiny part that craved his attention more than anything.

"Please. Jack. Oh, God."

He pulled her closer, until everything came into contact with his mouth all at once and her legs draped over his shoulders as he finally gave her what she wanted. Her back arched, and she couldn't stop herself from using the soles of her feet to push closer to that incredible source of pleasure. He didn't disappoint, his lips surrounding her and sucking gently—tongue rubbing against her.

That was all it took. She grabbed a breath and

then let go with a loud moan, pumping herself against him as her body flashed red-hot, the lights in the room fading to almost nothing. Again and again her inner walls clamped, finding nothing to grab onto, and yet the ecstasy was still stronger than anything she'd experienced in her life.

She lay there for a few seconds, mouth open, eyes closed, her lungs snatching for air and still feeling deprived.

When random thoughts finally started trickling back into her brain, she was stunned. Winded. Unnerved. Then she looked down to find his eyes on her, his mouth still poised between her legs.

She couldn't believe she'd let him do that to her. On a hotel-room bar, of all things. But she couldn't bring herself to regret it.

"You're bad," she said, unable to come up with a more sophisticated expression at the moment. "Very, very bad."

He laughed and stood, reaching behind her— to help her down, she thought. She was wrong. Snap went the clasp on her bra, and he eased her upright, removing the garment before he finally gave her a response.

"Sweetheart, you have no idea just how bad I can be."

CHAPTER NINE

HE SCRABBLED FRANTICALLY *at the heavy lid, trying to pry it open. How could she breathe inside there?*

She couldn't.

Putting the tips of his fingers beneath the smooth, shiny surface, he put all his force into opening it, breath whistling out through his teeth, muscles shaking with exertion as he strained upwards. His grip failed, hands slipping and throwing him back onto the plush carpet behind him. Soft music played in the background and people milled around, holding plates piled with food.

Why wasn't anyone helping him? Couldn't they see she was trapped?

He glanced around for something. Anything. His eyes fell on a crowbar that had been tossed up against the wall beside a dainty blue velvet couch. Crawling toward it, he grabbed it with both hands, the weight of it surprising him. He stood to his feet, dragging the metal bar behind him until he was in front of the box once again. The music got louder, and what had been soothing elevator music became a little more sinister in tone. Nothing that he could put his finger on exactly as it seemed to be the same tune.

Time was running out.

It was as if everyone else had finally noticed as well. They gathered around him, plates in hand, as he swung the heavy crowbar up, like he would one of those carnival hammers, and somehow got it to hook under the lid. He swallowed, suddenly not so sure about what he was doing. But they were all watching now. Waiting. Including a familiar blonde near the back of the room.

Where had he seen her before?

He shrugged and turned back to his task. Taking a deep breath, he silently counted to three.

One...two...

Three!

He put his full weight onto the metal rod, pushing down, down, down, the splintering of wood telling him he was getting somewhere. With a groan the top released and popped up an inch or two before the crowbar fell out of the groove. But no matter, he'd broken whatever seal was holding it closed.

He dropped the tool beside him and once again placed his fingers beneath the lid and slowly lifted. The sheen of blue satin met his eyes, the color matching that of the sofa behind him. He pushed the top higher and saw the cool white skin of her cheek. Her nose. Her pale lips.

A shot of horror went through him as he finished opening the top of the box.

It wasn't Paula. And she wasn't sleeping.
Mira!

He let go of the lid, and it fell in a series of disjointed frames, like a stack of still shots ruffled with a thumb to form movement. Then it hit the lower half of the box with a craaack!

Jack jerked, his eyelids flying apart and meeting darkness. Panic swept through him. He reached next to him to see if Paula was still there. His fingers met warm flesh, and he let his head drop back to the pillow in relief.

Just a dream.

More thoughts sifted through. Memories of making love. Groaning as he'd touched each silky inch of her body. Trying to hold off the inevitable until it had become too much, and he hadn't been able to resist pouring himself into her. Holding her until his breathing had slowed.

He swallowed hard, his head turning to the left. But it hadn't been Paula.

It had been Mira last night.

It was still Mira this morning.

And he'd enjoyed himself far too much. Had laughed and played the wicked rogue to the very end.

Hell.

He threw his arm over his eyes and tried to figure exactly what had happened last night.

A fling.

Yes. She'd used that word. So had he, in his head.

The bed shifted as she moved. Sighed.

Jack couldn't resist turning his head again. It was morning, it had to be, but it was still some time before dawn, judging from the darkness that hovered around the edges of the curtains. His adjusting eyes caught the first glimpse of a bare shoulder peeking from beneath the thick duvet cover. Her back was to him, her arm curled up to rest on the pillow beside her face.

The face he'd just seen lying in a satin-lined coffin.

Damn. And his bottle of sleeping pills sat on the bedside table untouched. The "mess" he'd been worried about her seeing.

He swung his legs out of bed and sat on the edge of the mattress for several long seconds, trying to stamp out the images still flickering in his mind. To distract himself, he opened the drawer on the table and knocked the medicine inside it. No need to let Mira see them. She'd just ask questions.

Questions he couldn't answer.

Like why he'd put her in Paula's place. The dream was the same as always, but the face had changed.

It had to be the aftereffects of the avalanche. Of those people suffocating, and one of them dying. Mira had been there, so maybe that's why she'd been in the nightmare this time. His wife's coffin had been closed. In reality, there hadn't been a body to go in it as Paula had been incinerated along with most of the other passengers.

Or maybe Mira had been in his dream because his subconscious was telling him to slam the lid down on this particular relationship and to seal it tight. But they didn't have a relationship.

They had a fling.

Just the word had a calming effect on him.

He'd had fun. There was no crime in that.

So why did he feel like the lowest form of low?

Guilt, probably. A false sense of loyalty to a woman he'd loved and lost.

She'd want you to go on.

Yes, she would. But that's not what he wanted. He remembered all too well facing that polished coffin and wondering how he was going to pick himself up and go on living.

Never again.

Standing, he made his way to the bathroom, suddenly wishing they'd gone to her room instead. Then he could just quietly get dressed and let himself out. No awkward goodbyes. No wondering if you should say thank you or I'm sorry.

He took his time, brushing his teeth and show-ering, then toweling off, all the time rehearsing exactly what he was going to say when he opened that door. But all he could see was the way Mira's back had arched like a cat as she'd moaned.

Please, don't stop.

Yes, he'd made her say it again. And where male pride should be, there was a slight sense of something else. Shame?

No.

He wasn't sure what the emotion was, but he didn't like it. It felt like something was poised to break loose, like that snow on the mountain that had gotten heavier and heavier until it had finally thundered down that slope, wiping away anyone in its path.

And from what Jack could see, he was stand-ing right in front of it. Only it wasn't snow. But something just as devastating.

Staring at himself in the mirror, he wrapped a towel around his waist, wishing he'd thought to bring in a fresh set of clothes. Getting dressed would send an obvious hint that the night was over and that it was time to make their way back to reality and their own separate beds.

Except that tiny images of the pleasure he'd given and received last night circled in his head, bringing with them a whole new set of ideas. Ones that whispered that this was only a fling, no need to fear. Just get back in there and do a little more flinging.

The more he thought about it the more he relaxed. Why not? He wanted her. Wanted to slide his hands over that lithe body and roll her beneath him again. She'd seemed to like it as much as he had. In fact, there was a sore spot on his shoulder he was pretty sure had been made by Mira's nails as they'd reached yet another pinnacle.

Yes. He wanted that. Wanted more of those scratches. More of those kisses.

It was okay. The dream had been nothing more than the stupid workings of his mind and that avalanche.

He undid the towel and let it drop to the floor, his body already anticipating what he wanted to do to her next.

Sweetheart, I hope you're ready.

He turned out the bathroom light so it wouldn't disturb her, then carefully opened the door. He was halfway across the room when he realized the bed seemed a little flatter than it had been. He frowned, moving closer. It looked different because it *was* different.

Mira was no longer there under the covers. His eyes skated around the room, going through the door to the living area and seeing just a silent hotel room.

No sound. No flash of movement.

He glanced at the floor next to the bed. No clothes. Although his were now folded and placed neatly on the seat of a chair on the other side of the room.

She was gone.

She'd done exactly what he would have done had he woken up in her room that morning. She'd crept out of bed and thrown on her clothes while he'd been in the bathroom. And then she'd turned tail and raced as fast as she could out of the door and out of his life.

* * *

Sleep with him, she'd said. *It'll do you both good,* she'd said.

Mira slammed her hairbrush down on the small vanity in her room and berated herself for running away like a coward. It would have been better to just lie there and pretend to be asleep, and then when Jack came back into the room give a big stretch as if she'd just woken up. She could have nonchalantly said she had to get dressed for work and say, "Thanks for everything."

Yeah, like propping her up on the bar and making her see stars.

In reality, she hadn't slept a wink once they'd made love a second time—in his bed this time. She'd lain awake for hours, totally blown away by what had happened between them. Rather than kick the attraction in the teeth and send it skidding down the road, it was now crouched in the left-hand corner of her mirror, grinning at her with that all-knowing smile. No matter how many times she blinked, it was still there.

Maybe because the smile belonged to the

stuffed Cheshire cat Ellory had sent her for her birthday last year.

"Yeah. Keep grinning and it's under the bed for you."

When the smile remained where it was, she found the corners of her own mouth lifting. "Oh, Ellory. What have I done?"

But, of course, her friend wasn't there to tell her what she should do the morning after.

She wanted to see him again. Something she hadn't expected.

Gulping, she scrubbed her hand over her stomach. She was going to go and get all attached to him, she just knew it.

"Idiot."

She laid her head down on the dressing table and thought through all the options.

Option one: she could remain in her room for the next two weeks…or however long he was scheduled to be here.

Option two: she could wear a Gaga-ish mask and pretend she was musical royalty.

Option three: she could forget about this whole bet-slash-resolution thing.

But she knew Ellory would worry about her if she really did go and jump into a new relationship. Hell, she would be worried about herself, if it came to that. She had three failed relationships under her belt. *Serious* relationships. To jump into a new one almost on the heels of breaking her engagement to Robert…

Stupid.

Which brought her back to thinking up more options.

She yawned. Option four: she could fall asleep and hope she didn't wake up for a couple of weeks.

Or she could just be a grown-up and go up to him and say, "Hey. Thanks for last night. I had a lot of fun. See ya around."

Quick. To the Point. Truthful.

She liked it.

She dragged herself up off the chair and headed to the bed, crinkling her nose at Chessie, who was still grinning madly at her. She knocked him sideways.

There. Just grin into the pillow for a while.

She decided to jump in the shower and try to

pull herself together. As soon as she stepped under the spray she knew it was the right thing to do. The warm water helped soothe her nerves. Maybe she really would take a nap. Everything looked worse when you were tired. Scrubbing herself down with a soapy loofah, she tried to put what had happened last night out of her mind.

If she could just get his scent off her body and out of her head...

From a distance she heard her cell ring.

Please, don't be Jack. Not right now.

Despite her thoughts, by the second ring she'd sluiced off the rest of the soap and stepped out of the shower, feet slipping for a second on the bare tile floor in her hurry to get to the phone.

Damn, damn, damn.

She picked up the thing and glanced at the read-out, adding a fourth "damn" for good measure. Robert. Not Jack.

"Hello?"

"Mira, are you free?"

Oh, Lord. Now what? If he thought they were getting back together he was mistaken. "Why?"

"Number Five is up here with me, and he might need some help."

"Jack? What happened?" Her heart started crashing around in her chest, making her vision swim for a second or two. Here she was agonizing over what they'd done last night, and he was already up on the slopes first thing this morning.

"He's fine. But someone fell off the ski lift and…uh…Dr. Perry says she has multiple broken bones. Can you get up here? EMS has already been called, but it'll be a little while, there's evidently a lot of ice after the freeze we had yesterday, and they're having to deal with some accidents on the roads. Your guy wants to stabilize the guest and then get her someplace warmer."

"On my way. Which slope?" She probably already knew. Jack wouldn't risk his life on one of the bigger ones.

"Grade two." There was a pause. "Mira, we think she was a jumper. There were a couple of witnesses who saw her go over."

Her heart stuttered.

A jumper. Oh, God. Every couple of years

someone decided life was too painful to bear and threw themselves off the lifts and onto the slopes in a suicide attempt. Normally it was onto one of the more advanced slopes, though, as the lifts servicing those areas went higher.

Her throat was so tight she wasn't sure she'd be able to respond. But when she opened her mouth, somehow the words were there. "Give me a few minutes. I'll keep my cell with me, so call if there's any change."

Throwing the phone onto the bed, she rushed around yanking her clothes on and then her snow pants and parka. Her coat still had a ripped spot on the sleeve—just like the shredded portion of her heart.

Please, let her be okay.

She searched around for her gloves for a minute or two, and then frowned at the unfamiliar pair she found in her pocket.

Jack's gloves. He'd given them to her after the avalanche yesterday.

Her throat tightened further.

Had that just been yesterday? It seemed like it had happened weeks ago.

In reality, there were plenty of accidents to go around at a ski resort, but not usually on a day when she'd gotten so little sleep. Although, with the adrenaline now coursing through her veins, she felt wide awake. Her hair was still wet, but it would have to stay that way for now. She hauled it back into a quick bun and secured a rubber band around it. She'd just pull a hat on and then her parka hood over the top of that. She could blow-dry it when she got back to her room later.

She knocked Chessie back upright. "Watch the room for me, okay?"

Five minutes later, she hurried out the door, telling the front desk where to reach her. She snapped on her skis. It would be faster to go up the lift and then ski down to their position. Slope number two. A little harder than the bunny slope but still an easy ride for beginners like Jack.

Sliding past those in line with an occasional murmured "Excuse me", along with the fact that there was a medical emergency on one of the slopes, she cut to the front and allowed the next chair to scoop her up and carry her on her way. Her eyes scanned the area. There. About halfway up there was a small crowd of about five people. The one at the center of the group, nearest the patient, was Jack, the sun glinting off the lighter strands of his hair.

Her heart squeezed again.

At least the injured woman had someone capable helping her. As a sports medicine doctor he'd have specialized in orthopedics and be well versed on serious breaks. There could be no better person attending that patient, and that included her.

Impatient to get down there, she had to wait another three or four minutes for the lift to reach the top of the slope. Then she was off and with a couple of pushes from her poles was heading down the mountain at a good clip, mentally playing through her mind how far she had to go before she reached the scene. Thankfully the trip down was a lot faster than the trip up. She turned her body and skis sideways and skidded to a halt next to the little group.

Robert nodded at her from the edge of the ring, where his job was to keep gawkers at bay. She'd really have to say something to him about using

Number Five when referring to Jack. Yeah, yeah, she'd referred to him that way in her head as well, but that was so she could keep some emotional distance.

A lot of good that had done.

Right now, though, that was the least of her worries.

She knelt beside him, noting that he had several splints laid out and was currently binding one to the patient's arm. The girl— Oh, Lord, and that's all she was. A teenager. On her back, with her eyes open wide, she whimpered in pain as Jack worked on her. The sleeves on both her jacket and her sweater had been slashed up past her right elbow, revealing a bloody spot on her forearm that looked ominous.

Compound fracture. A hint of pearly bone protruded from the site.

Dragging in a shuddered breath, she murmured, "What have you got?"

He glanced up, and his lips tightened for a second then he said, "Stacy Painter, sixteen. Broken right radius, compound at the ulna, and two fractured femurs—both at the neck, from what

I can guess, based on her leg position. And she has tenderness on her right side as well…possible fractured ribs."

She closed her eyes at the mention of the femur fractures. "At the neck" meant the bones had broken off at the ball where they went into the socket. And if those sections went too long without oxygen, it could mean a double hip replacement. In a teenage girl.

Now wasn't the time to think of that, though. They needed to have her ready to transport once the EMS crew arrived. "What do you want me to do?"

"I'm stabilizing the compound fracture and need to protect it. But I've got her radius and hips to deal with." He glanced up at her again. "We have to do this without any meds. Can you talk to her while I work?"

No pain meds. She knew that was protocol when they didn't know what a patient's other injuries might be, but it had to agonizing for Stacy to have Jack manipulate her bones. It was one of the worst parts of being a doctor. Once again, she found herself glad he was there.

She didn't argue about what he'd asked her to do. Didn't say she was a doctor too so she should be doing some of the work. She simply scooched over until she was by the girl's head and then leaned down. "Hi, Stacy. My name is Mira. Dr. Perry is going to get you all fixed up."

The girl blinked, a few tears breaking free and sliding down her cheeks. Then her eyes focused on Mira. "He—he said to call him Jack."

Mira glanced up to find that the man's eyes were on her. She pulled her attention back to the patient. "Is that so?" She forced a smile. "You're lucky. He doesn't let just anyone call him that."

In fact, some of us call him Number Five.

She pushed that little voice away and continued. "What happened?"

The girl's chin wobbled and another tear escaped. She wouldn't quite meet her eyes. "I—I fell. Off the ski lift."

Had she hesitated before using the word "fell" or was that her imagination?

There were witnesses.

Mira glanced up at the chairs going overhead—people in them were now staring at the scene below. It seemed like a long way down from here. The teen had to have tumbled a few feet once she hit, to have broken so many bones.

"Was the safety bar down on your seat?"

The girl winced as Jack touched her leg. "No. I—I forgot."

Another coincidence.

Oh, honey, what would drive you to do something like this?

She forced out her next words. "Do you know where your parents are?" Had anyone contacted them yet?

Stacy started to shake her head and then screamed, the sound ending on a group of sobs.

Jack had slid a long splint beneath her right leg and hip and was strapping it in place.

Sliding onto her side, so that her head was as close to Stacy's as possible and blocking the view of what Jack was doing, she said, "I know it's painful, honey. Dr…er, Jack is putting something called splints on your legs so they won't hurt as bad once the ambulance comes." Mira wanted to squeeze her hand, do something to comfort her, but she couldn't. The girl had bones broken in both arms. She settled for murmuring to her instead.

The girl closed her eyes for a few seconds and then opened them again, looking at Mira. "It was so stupid, you know?"

Jumping? Oh, God...

She was afraid to ask. Afraid the girl would clam up. So she settled for asking her earlier question again, while Jack secured her leg. "I know. Can you tell me where your parents are?"

"At home. I'm here with my cheerleading squad."

A cheerleader. It just kept getting worse. An injury like this could be life-changing for anyone, even more so for a high-school girl who needed strength and agility in order to do something she loved.

Down below, the sound of a siren came through.

Thank God. The EMS team was here sooner than she'd expected, despite the icy road conditions. She touched Jack's shoulder. He didn't look up from what he was doing but said, "I hear them. I want to get this other leg in place so they can take her right away."

He glanced up, his eyes meeting hers. Mira saw her own fear and horror reflected back in his gaze. "Last one. Can you keep her calm?" he asked.

"We'll be fine."

He nodded then pulled a second long splint toward the girl. Thank heavens her father kept a full array of those on the premises for times like this.

"Get ready." He took hold of the teen's leg to stabilize it.

"Ahhhh!" The agonized shriek tore right through Mira's insides, leaving her trembling. "It hurts," the girl sobbed. "It hurts so bad."

Mira touched her cheek. "I know, he's almost done." At least the pain brought with it a little good news. Stacy had feeling in her legs, so her spinal cord was intact. If she had landed differently she could be paralyzed or worse.

She glanced up to see if Robert was still there. He was. Watching over the proceedings with a brooding expression. No time to worry about that now. "Robert, can you go find one of the girls' chaperones—?"

"Th-there aren't any." Stacy bit her lip. "A friend got us some driver's licenses. We came on our own."

Another layer of shock pressed down on her chest. "*None* of your parents know you're here? How many of you are there?"

"Five." She turned her head away. "Th-they think we're at a training camp."

This was bad. Very bad. That meant there were no "permission to treat" forms on file. No adults to give verbal permission. "Are you all the same age?"

Stacy nodded. "We skipped school yesterday. We're planning to go back tomorrow. But m-my boyfriend called to break up with me a few hours ago." She closed her eyes again. "So stupid. I thought it would change things."

Change things? As in her boyfriend might decide he didn't want to break up with her if he heard she'd tried to jump from a ski-lift?

Although on the one hand that made no sense, at least the girl seemed to acknowledge she shouldn't have done whatever it was.

She motioned to Jack to wait. He frowned, but

stopped with the second splint still a few inches from the teen's leg.

"What's your phone number, honey?" They needed to get in touch with her parents...or someone. Soon.

Stacy gave it to her, and Mira wrote it in the snow with her gloved finger. "You aren't going to tell them about any of this, are you?"

Any of this. The girls' secret little trip to the mountains? Or Stacy's fall?

"They're going to be happy you're safe." It was the only answer she could give at the moment that wouldn't upset her. Because, yes, the parents needed to know, as did the authorities. Especially if she really had attempted suicide. Although Mira hoped she was reading the girl right and that it had been a bid for attention from her boyfriend. Either way, she needed counseling.

"Do you think so?"

"Yes." That was what was important right now.

She underlined the digits she'd written in the snow then fixed her attention on Robert. "Can you read that?"

He nodded.

"See if you can find the rest of her group. And get a hold of her parents."

"Okay." He hesitated. "After this, we need to talk."

"Just find her parents. Nothing else matters right now."

Out of the corner of her eye she saw Jack's hands tighten on the splint and wondered what he was thinking. What she'd said was true. Nothing else mattered right now, except for treating their patient. She took a deep breath and murmured to the girl, laying a hand on her forehead, "Jack has to finish securing your leg. Are you ready?"

The EMS guys were already trudging up the slope, one pulling a stretcher, while the other one carried a medical kit.

"Yes."

She nodded at Jack then looked at Stacy. "Keep your eyes on mine. It'll be over with in just a minute."

Behind her came the sound of something sliding on the snow. The splint as it went under her leg.

Stacy's head went back and she cried out, the

hoarse scream rising along with the level of pain. Mira's eyes watered, despite the number of times she'd worked on injuries like this. But never on a minor who was up here all alone. Or one who'd decided being without her boyfriend had called for drastic—and very possibly permanent—measures. Mira smoothed the girl's hair as she settled into wrenching sobs once again.

She herself had made a drastic change, in the form of a resolution, because of what had happened with Robert. But never in her darkest moments had she thought of ending her life.

"Done." Jack's low word made her draw a relieved breath.

"The worst is over, Stacy." At least physically. Any other treatment would happen with pain medication at the hospital. But once her parents found out what the teen had done, the emotional pain would begin—along with healing, hopefully. The resort was required to report any suspected suicide attempts, which meant Stacy would receive a psychological evaluation at some point. She hoped the girl got the help she desperately needed.

The paramedics arrived, and Jack explained the situation while Mira stayed with the girl, talking to her. Jack had hoped to get her down to the hotel where it was warm, but at least this way she'd only have to be moved once.

The rescue workers secured Stacy's neck in case there were other injuries and gently slid her from the snow onto the rescue stretcher. Up on skids, the lightweight plastic frame would stabilize her back and keep Stacy off the snow, while allowing it to be pulled rather than carried, like a traditional stretcher.

Mira snapped her skis back on and spoke in a low voice to Jack. "I need to go down and see about the other girls. I think we'll need to call in child services."

Jack nodded. "I'll go with her to the hospital." He moved over to Mira and slid his fingers beneath her chin. He had gloves on—he must have rented them, because she was wearing his. "And then I'm going to come knocking on your door. And you're going to tell me exactly why I have the number five attached to me wherever I go. And what it means."

With that he was gone. Back at Stacy's side, helping fill the workers in on what he'd done and what he suspected.

Leaving Mira to ski the rest of the way down the hill and wonder exactly how she was going to tell him that he was man number five in a long line of men. And hope he'd understand why she now had to move on to number six.

CHAPTER TEN

A RESOLUTION.

Jack wasn't sure he'd heard her correctly. "What kind of resolution?"

In Mira's hotel room, he listened as she told him about what she and the blonde had decided to do for their New Year's resolutions.

"So…" His jaw hardened to stone. After five hours of sitting at the hospital while Stacy's parents drove up from Aspen to be with her, this wasn't what he'd expected to hear. "Sleeping with me was just part of some…*hilarious* New Year's prank."

"Oh, it was no prank." Her eyes skipped away from his. "And what happened between us wasn't supposed to happen at all."

Seated on her bed, clutching some kind of weird stuffed animal, he felt like he'd been sucker-punched, landing in some crazy dream sequence. One that was almost worse than his periodic nightmares.

"So you're only planning on dating twenty-five men. Not sleeping with every single one of them."

"Correction. I wasn't going to sleep with *any* of them."

Jack wasn't sure if he should be pleased she'd made an exception in his case or insulted. "Maybe I would have been better off going with Mrs. Botox last week. It would have been a whole lot less complicated."

A flash of what might have been hurt swept through her eyes before she blinked it away. "Maybe you should have."

Hell. This was not how he'd wanted this talk to go down. But never in his wildest imaginings had he thought she'd gone out with him as part of some cockamamie scheme to date as many men as possible over the course of a year.

"Why did you decide on this for your resolution?"

"I was hurt. I didn't want to get involved with anyone after what happened with Robert."

"Your broken engagement."

She hesitated and then nodded.

"So you thought this was an acceptable alternative."

"No. It was a spur-of-the moment thing. Ellory and I have a tradition…" She shifted the animal on her lap. "Never mind. Anyway, she didn't think I could see it through to the end, thought I'd get stuck part way through."

"Really? It looks like you're doing pretty damn well to me." Good. Anger. At least that was an emotion he was well acquainted with. He grabbed it with both hands. "Exactly when were you planning on telling me about it?"

Mira's teeth came down on her lip.

Ah, so she hadn't planned on telling him at all. "Were you going to tell any of them?"

"No." The word came out as a whisper.

The thought of her parading around with three or four more men while he was still at the resort made his gut roll around inside him, although he wasn't sure why he cared. Probably just part of his male pride. As much as he didn't want to get involved with anyone on a permanent basis—in that, he and Mira were definitely alike—he also hadn't liked the way her ex had said he wanted to talk to her.

He wondered what the man thought about what Mira was doing. Robert evidently knew about it, had actually called him by a damned number rather than by his name.

And that just made his anger burn brighter. Hotter.

"So it was okay for your ex-fiancé to know and get a couple of good chuckles out of it. I'm surprised you didn't give each of us a hand stamp. A kind of one-day pass into your magic kingdom."

She stood, dropping the stuffed cat onto the bed. "It wasn't supposed to be like that. It wasn't a joke. At least, not to me. I was trying to avoid being hurt again. Trying not to repeat the same mistakes."

Isn't that what he'd done—avoided getting involved with anyone to keep from losing them? But he hadn't decided to go out with a million different women in order to achieve that goal. He'd avoided going out with any of them, for the most part.

"So how does your ex know about any of this?"

She shrugged. "I think he heard me talking to Ellory about it at the bar one day."

"He wants you back, you know."

"He doesn't. Not really. He only thinks he does now that he can't have me." Her chin went up. "Remember that lady who came on to you? She and Robert are well acquainted."

That made him blink. Her ex had been with that bimbo? "You know that for a fact?"

"I didn't see them going at it, if that's what you mean. One of the female instructors saw them making out in a supply shed. When I confronted him, he admitted to it. And then I found out there were others—some of them his students." Her eyes swam for a second before she forced back the remembered humiliation of breaking off their engagement amid the swirling rumors.

"Bastard."

"That goes without saying." She gave a hard smile. "But it's happened to me with more than one man. Since I seem incapable of telling the good guys from the bad, I figured it would be better if I stuck to 'shallow and meaningless' when it comes to dating. This year was supposed to show me how that's done."

It didn't make him feel any better that she lumped him into the shallow and meaningless category. "So, I'm man number five."

"Don't call yourself that."

"That's what you called me, isn't it? And your friend. And your ex."

"You're right. I'm sorry."

He picked up a hat on the table, the pink one she wore when out on the snow. "Are you going to date other men over the next couple of weeks? While I'm still here?"

"I don't know. It's not like I pick up a new guy every night."

No, but he doubted she had a lot of trouble attracting them. The woman was gorgeous. And smart. And her ex was an asshole above all others.

He suddenly knew what he was going to do.

"What if I asked you to stick to me for the remainder of my stay?" He wasn't sure why, but if she was going to have random dates with random men, then he wanted to be the guy she went out with more than once. More than twice.

"I'm not sure what you mean."

He set her hat down then moved toward her, sliding his hands along her cheeks and easing her face up. "I want you to date me. Just a group of outings, nothing serious. You can show me the sights—when you're not on duty, of course. I'll get the vacation my coach was looking for, and you'll get a man who's not interested in passing anything but the time."

The words tasted bitter on his tongue as they passed over it, as if he were asking her to be a paid escort or something. He wasn't.

But he couldn't promise her any more than that. They were from different worlds. His wife had left a thriving practice to be with him. He'd taken her not only from the children she'd treated in California but from every sick kid who might have come under her care in the future.

He would never ask that of anyone again.

"Why would you want to do that?" Mira asked.

"For exactly the reasons I mentioned."

"You're not mad about the whole number thing?"

He wouldn't go so far as to say that. "It's not what I expected but, then again, not much in this life is."

"Remind me how long you'll be here."

He calculated the days in his head. "I have to go back in a little less than two weeks." And why did his stay suddenly seem far too short?

Because the trip was working?

Or because he was an idiot?

She paused for several seconds and stared just beyond his face as if doing some heavy thinking. "These wouldn't be real dates. Just going around together and seeing the sights."

Letting go of her, he nodded. "If that's how you prefer to think of it, I'm okay with that." He caught her eye. "But you can't move on to number six until after I'm gone."

"Okay." She stepped closer and touched his arm. "For what it's worth, I'm sorry. You weren't just a number last night."

The words went a long way toward soothing

his bruised pride. "For what it's worth, neither were you."

And that was exactly what he was afraid of. His strange dream came back to him in all its horrifying detail. The fact that Mira's face had been the one he'd seen in that coffin seemed like a clear warning: *This is what could happen if you allow yourself to get too involved.*

Rational or not, it was the truth.

So what was he doing here, asking her to see him exclusively? Exactly what he'd said. It was time he poked his head back out into the world. Last night had at least shown him that much. He'd had a genuinely good time. And his reasons for sleeping with her hadn't been a whole lot purer than hers had been. He'd been upset by that death up on the slope, and so he'd turned to her in order to escape for a few hours. Wasn't that was she was doing? Trying to escape a painful situation?

He could act all holier than thou about her resolution, but the reality was right there in front of him.

"So. If we're going to do this, what would you like to see first?"

How about what was under those clothes?

He wasn't going to say it, even if it was what he was thinking. And he already knew what she looked like naked. It seemed that having her last night had not quenched his thirst. In fact, the memories of them together just served to make him feel even more parched. So he would just ignore the feeling and hope it went away.

"Well, I didn't get a chance to see the rest of the property, since I wasn't exactly concentrating during our sleigh ride."

She smiled. "I think I can remedy that."

"Another sleigh ride?" One brow hiked up. He didn't see how their ride would fare any better this time than it did last time.

"How about a ride without the sleigh?"

No way was he touching that one.

"If you're talking about on horseback, I don't know how to ride."

"Wow. You don't? You don't know how to ski. You don't know how to ride. Were you born in a monastery or something?" She stepped up close and tilted her head back. "Don't worry. While

I do have some horses in mind, they don't have four legs."

"Really? Then what do they have?"

She smiled. "I have some things I need to get done today, and I want to check with my father on something, but if you're up for it I'll show you exactly what I mean first thing tomorrow morning.

Mira revved up the snowmobile. Owned by her dad, she'd often used it to get away from the crowds and go off by herself. There were a series of private trails that only she and the other employees knew about.

She and Robert had ridden around a couple of times, but he'd always been in the driver's seat when they'd been together. But this time she was the one in front. Jack didn't know how to ride one of these either. He was a warm-climate boy through and through.

"Put your helmet on and climb aboard!"

Looking the slightest bit dubious, Jack slid the helmet onto his head and fastened the strap before swinging a leg over the back of the vehicle. "You're sure you know how to drive this."

"I've done it my whole life."

He chuckled. "You are just full of surprises."

"Am I? You have no idea." She let go of the steering-wheel to fasten her own strap. "Ready? You're going to want to hang on tight."

His hands went to her waist as she eased them away from the equipment barn, skirting the ski-lift area. His grip reminded her of the way he'd lifted her onto that bar. She had to fight to banish the image from her mind and concentrate.

The two ski-lift attendants waved at her as she went by. Mira waved back. Maneuvering down a slight incline, she rode onto a section of the property that was partially wooded but which had a path carved out of it.

"Where are we going?" he asked, above the roar of the motor.

"I know a little place." She'd let her father know she'd be gone for the day—possibly until tomorrow, depending on how things went. And in the back of the snowmobile she'd packed a lunch, along with wine and a thick blanket. There was firewood at their destination, but it could still get pretty chilly. "Okay, I'm going to crank it up a bit."

Mira pressed the accelerator lever with her thumb and the track on the bottom of the vehicle picked up speed, grabbing onto the snow and propelling them forward. The destination she had in mind was about five miles away through some of the most gorgeous country known to man. Jack settled in closer, his body molding to hers from behind, legs pressed tight to hers. Was he doing that on purpose?

"This is similar to a Jet Ski," he yelled in her ear. "Except we push water through the engine to propel us forward."

"Never ridden on one."

"You'd like it."

Yeah, she probably would. Too bad he'd never teach her how to ride one. Or a surfboard, for that matter.

That's not in the cards, Mira. Just enjoy today.

Silence reigned between them for a few moments as they ate up some more terrain. She slowed to go around a tree and then accelerated once again, the tracks kicking up a blast of snow.

When she'd begun her yearlong journey to become footloose and fancy-free, she never dreamed she'd wind up riding on her dad's snow-mobile with one of her dates. Or making out on a sleigh ride. Or working side by side to rescue avalanche victims.

Or helping a girl with emotional wounds much deeper than her own.

She and Jack worked well together. Which was probably why it was harder just to mosey on past him. During their confrontation yesterday he'd seemed offended that he was just a number on a list in her head, and he was right. She knew there might be a blip or two but hadn't expected to crash and burn quite so soon.

And that was the problem. She had no idea whether she should keep on trying to do some-thing that seemed to be against her nature. Or if she should just forfeit her bet and agree with El-lory that this had been a royally bad idea.

She could pay up and be done.

With Jack's arms wrapped around her waist, it was easy to imagine just snuggling down in the here and now and enjoy their remaining time together.

His helmet bumped against hers once as she made another turn, re-emphasizing just how close he was. Maybe she should bypass the cabin and just keep driving around for the rest of the afternoon. She was enjoying have him next to her just a little too much.

But all too soon the small log building came into view.

Her parents' original home, and the place she'd been born.

Her dad had kept it to remind himself of where he'd come from. She could probably live out here, rather than at the hotel, but she preferred to visit the cabin periodically as a treat. She knew all too well how mundane the things in life could become if you weren't careful.

Like her and Robert's relationship? So it would seem. At least on his part.

Looking back, though, she wondered if that spark had really been there to begin with, or if she'd assumed that since they'd had so much in common their similarities would see them through.

Pulling up to the front door, she used the hand-brake to stop. Jack hesitated and then let go of her and climbed off. She started to follow, swinging one leg over the front, then sat sideways on the seat instead, looking up at him while she tried to re-gather her composure.

"So how was your first snowmobile ride? Did you like it?"

He gave her sideways smile. "It was interesting."

She'd expected a little more enthusiasm than that. Then again, Jack seemed to have cornered the market on measured reactions. That's why his behavior in his hotel room had shocked her so much. Who would have known he had a bit of caveman wandering around inside him.

And on that note she'd better shut down this line of thought before it got her into trouble.

"Okay." She laughed. "We'll go with interesting." She stood up and opened a storage compartment in the back of the snowmobile and pulled out a small chest containing their lunch. Jack took it from her with a raised brow.

"I thought you might be hungry." She tugged the blanket from the compartment as well, draping it over her arm.

"I might." He nodded toward the cabin. "I didn't know this was out here. Is it yours?"

"No. It belongs to the fam…to my dad."

"He doesn't rent it out?"

She paused. "He likes to come out here to stay every once in a while."

"He and your mother are divorced."

She headed for the cabin, peeling off her gloves and checking her pocket for the key to the front door. "They are." She and her dad had made their peace last week, but there were still some tender spots when it came to the reasons for her parents' divorce.

"Sorry." His voice came from behind her. "Is your mother still living?"

"Mmm-hmm. She lives in Aspen. How about your parents? Still living?"

"Yes. They live on the east coast of Florida."

She stuck the key in the lock and turned. "Let me guess. They live on the beach too?"

Jack laughed. "How did you know?"

"Surfer dude. Plenty of beach knowledge and almost no mountain knowledge. You had to have gotten it from somewhere."

He followed her into the house and looked around. "Wow. Not what I expected."

Mira peered at the interior of her parents' old home and tried to see it through his eyes. Rustic on the outside, the house was modest but modern. Hardwood floors ran throughout the cabin, and her dad had done most of the work inside himself, from the plank walls to the oak trim. There were so many memories attached to this place. Some of them good. Some of them not so good.

"Not quite as swanky as the lodge, is it?"

"It's not that." He moved over to the oversized fireplace. "Does this work?"

"Dad keeps the wood box in here filled with split logs. The bigger chunks are outside. You'd be surprised how well it warms the place. Do you want to start a fire while I take our lunch into the kitchen?"

Mira took the basket and headed for the space across the room. The cabin was built on an open concept, so the dining and kitchen areas were all visible from the living room. And as she set the box down and gazed across the space, she couldn't help but admire Jack's strong back as he gathered wood from the compartment behind the wall and knelt in front of the fireplace.

By the time he had the fire going, she'd unloaded lunch, which consisted of fried chicken, potato salad, baked beans and some cheese and crackers. All hearty picnic food that would do well on the cold trip over here. She got out a pan for the beans and set it on the stove. "Do you want me to heat up the chicken, or do you prefer it cold?"

"I'll like whatever you do." His voice came from right behind her, making her jump.

She spun around. "You scared me."

"Join the crowd. You scare me too, lady." Something about the way he said it made her think he wasn't talking about being startled but about something a little deeper.

No. No *deeper* allowed. She'd lectured herself on this very thing. They'd only known each other for less than two weeks, but she was already feeling much too close to this man. It had to be the sex. Women felt an emotional response to sleeping with a man, right, whereas men could just shrug it off? At least, that's what she'd always heard. But maybe that wasn't always the case. Maybe Jack was struggling with some of the same issues she was.

She forced her voice to remain light. "Well, one thing that isn't scary is this lunch. Marie always makes a great fried chicken."

"Marie?"

"The chef at the lodge. She's been there ever since I was a teenager."

"You've lived here your whole life?" He unzipped his coat and moved around the bar, perching on one of the stools.

"My whole life. I lived with my mom for a year or two after the divorce but, yeah, I grew up here. Once I finished college and med school, I came back."

"Wow. I've always lived near the ocean, but my

parents moved around quite a bit. My dad was in the service. He retired in Florida."

Mira put the burner on low and turned around to face him. "My friend Ellory—the one from the resolution—likes to travel as well. She's been all over the place. But she grew up here too, her mom worked at the lodge when she was little."

"You can't see yourself doing that someday? Traveling?"

The funny thing was, lately she'd been thinking about that very thing. About whether it was time for her to spread her wings and move away from her childhood home. Make her own memories somewhere else. Maybe she'd stayed for so long to make peace with her dad. Now that she had, something inside her was itching with discontent.

"I went to college and medical school away from here, obviously. I don't know. It's certainly something to consider, but I'm not to that point yet. Maybe I just need to find a reason."

His jaw got tight. "Make sure that reason has to do with you, Mira. Not someone else."

Was he speaking from personal experience? Had he resented moving around as a kid?

She turned to stir the beans, the heat from the burner as well as the fireplace beginning to warm her. Shrugging out of her coat, she laid it over the bar behind her, deciding to ask. "Was it hard, moving from place to place when you were young?"

"What? Oh…" He shook his head. "No, that was just part of normal life—it didn't bother me. Anyway, you were right. The fireplace does a great job."

He picked up her coat and moved away from the bar, hanging their outerwear on the hooks her father had installed next to the door. Then he poked at the fire with his back to her.

Frowning, Mira gave the beans another couple of stirs as steam began to rise from the pot.

Make sure that reason has to do with you. Not someone else.

If he hadn't been talking about moving around during his childhood, then what? Had he moved as an adult because of someone else? No, he was a sports medicine doctor. He'd obviously taken the job in Texas because he'd wanted to—because he'd loved football and his team—not because someone had made him. But his coach had made him go on this vacation in the first place. Why?

She reached up to one of the overhead cabinets and pulled out two plates and wineglasses, rinsing and drying them. She did the same with the silverware in the drawer before setting everything on round twig placemats on the bar. "I think we're about ready."

When Jack joined her, she helped dish everything up and poured them each a glass of wine. "That fire feels good. Thanks."

"You're welcome." He pushed the food around on his plate for a minute or two. "You asked about it being hard to move. That wasn't what I meant about making sure you did it for yourself and not someone else."

Mira tensed, wondering where he was going with this and not sure she really wanted to know. "Okay."

"Did I tell you I was married at one time?"

Her eyes widened. She'd asked whether he was

married and when he'd said no, she'd just assumed he'd been single all his life. "No."

"I was. Paula was a pediatric oncologist with a thriving practice in California. She loved her patients. Her staff." He paused, staring at the handle of his fork as if it were suddenly fascinating. "Four years ago, I was approached by the Hawks and asked if I'd be their doctor. At the time I was working with a smaller team in California, so it would have been a big promotion for me. I asked Paula to go with me. Told her that with her skills she could open a practice anywhere in the U.S.—could keep helping sick kids, just like she did where she was."

Had the strain been too much, and they'd divorced over it? "Did she decide not to go?"

He shook his head. "Oh, she decided to go. But it would have been better if she hadn't."

"I don't understand."

Dropping his fork back onto his plate, he turned his stool to face her. "My wife got on the plane to fly out to Texas and never made it off." He took a deep breath. "It crashed in the Gulf of Mexico. Her body was never recovered."

CHAPTER ELEVEN

MIRA WAS SHOCKED.

He saw it in her face. But was she shocked at the fact that he'd been married or that his wife had died because of him?

Her fingers touched his. "God, Jack. I had no idea. I'm so sorry."

Yeah, well, so was he. Sorry he'd been so eager to climb up that career ladder. Sorry he'd dragged Paula with him as he'd gone up one step and then another without any thought as to how it would affect her career or the lives of her patients. Sorry that he never got to hold her and tell her that before she'd slipped away.

"I didn't tell you to gain your sympathy. I told you so you'd never make a decision you regretted."

She stared at him for several seconds, a bunch of emotions running over that beautiful face of hers. Then her mouth tipped to the side in a half-smile. "Too late. I've done plenty of things I've regretted."

"Like your ski instructor?"

Her brows went up, and her smile grew. "I'm sure you didn't mean that as in, 'Do you regret *doing* your ski instructor?' That does not sound good, Jack Perry."

Relief swept over him. She wasn't going to sit here and make him dissect his every regret or say that he shouldn't feel guilt over his wife's death. Or that he shouldn't take pills to sleep. She'd catalogued what he'd shared and was okay with moving past it. He was just as happy to keep the ball rolling in that direction.

"Well, how about this, then. Do you regret *doing* me?"

She drew imaginary circles on the wooden surface of the bar with her finger. "I think you have that event reversed, Doctor. I seem to remember *you* doing *me*."

"Is that so?" His body began to show a definite spark of interest in where this conversation was headed. "I think there was a little give-and-take going on there at the end."

"Your beans are getting cold," she said innocently, scooping up a bite of her own and popping it into her mouth.

He couldn't prevent a smile. "That's about the only thing getting cold." He'd indulge her. But now that she'd thrown open the door, he had no intention of slamming it shut again, agreement or no agreement.

Why not enjoy each other for the next week or so? There was nothing wrong with that, and as long as they were both okay with it...

So he dug into his own food with gusto. Putting off the inevitable would only make it that much sweeter. "What time do you have to be back?" He wanted to make sure he enjoyed every decadent second of their time together.

"Actually, I'm not due back until tomorrow, unless there's an emergency."

"I didn't pack clothes for an overnight stay."

Her lips pursed as she looked him over. "Who said you needed clothes?"

Okay, so there was no mistaking those words.

"Did you bring me out here just for this?" Not that he'd mind. At all.

"No, but now that we're here I'm thinking it might not be a bad idea. Unless you'd rather go back to the lodge."

Oh, sure. He was just going to smile and say, "Thanks but, no, thanks." Not hardly. Not with this particular woman.

"Going back is not on my agenda. In fact, my schedule just became wide open."

"Good, because I'm thinking the thick blanket I brought would look pretty darn good in front of the fire."

He picked up his chicken. "I can think of something else that would look even better." He took a bite, still staring at her.

"Mmm. So can I." She blew out a breath. "Wow. I don't know if Ellory is rubbing off on me or if it's you. I'm not usually this forward."

He swallowed his food, chasing it down with a slug of wine. "I like it. It's a whole lot easier knowing where you stand than having to guess."

That was one of the things that had bothered him most about Paula's death. He'd never been entirely sure whether she'd wanted to move to Texas or if she'd been doing it just to please him. The heart of his guilt lay in that uncertainty. If she hadn't wanted to come and had just spoken up, he would have stayed in California. Gladly. Now he'd never know. He pushed back the thought.

Mira sipped at her own wine. "It's funny. I've always been a good girl. Quiet. Obedient. It's why I love Ellory so much. She's spontaneous and fearless. She always goes after what she wants, rarely letting anything stand in her way."

"And you do?"

"Sometimes." Her mouth twisted. "I think I work too hard to meet other people's expectations of me. I forget who I am at times."

He set his glass down and touched a finger to her cheek. "I think you're the girl who's sitting at this bar right now. And the girl who worked so hard to rescue those people after the avalanche. There's more to you than you realize, Mira Dupris." His fingertip traveled along her jaw and then down her neck. "And you blow me away. Every time I look at you. Talk to you. I haven't been with many women since my wife's death. And never more than once, but with you..."

Taking a deep breath, he decided to go for broke. "But with you I find myself wanting a next time. And a next."

And maybe that revelation was where the healing finally began in earnest.

She gave a visible swallow then said, "I feel the same way. You were supposed to be just one more guy. But you're not."

He planted his hands on either side of her stool, gripping it tight and turning it toward him. Then he hauled it closer and leaned in. "I'm glad."

His mouth met hers and that familiar rush of heat washed over him, undiminished, just as strong as it had been the first time they'd kissed. That combination of sweet and sexy that went straight to his gut.

Hands touched the back of his neck and then curled around it as if afraid he was going to back away. Not likely. All he wanted was more.

Beneath her winter coat she'd worn a creamy turtleneck that, when he reached up to touch her, met his fingers with a buttery softness he wanted to lose himself in. Just like he wanted to lose himself in her. Skimming up her sides, he laid his palms on her back, luxuriating in the feel of her.

God, she just did it for him.

He didn't want to examine the whys right now, just wanted to enjoy being with her, absorb a little bit of that *joie de vivre* she had, just like a vampire.

Mira made a little sound in her throat, the kind that slid over a man like silk…that made him want to draw more of those sexy gasps and capture them inside his mouth.

"Hey," he whispered. "Let's break out that blanket."

She blinked at him with glazed eyes for a second before nodding and getting off the stool. She walked over to the sofa, and hell if his gaze didn't stick right to her ass, admiring every little twitch and jiggle it made as she moved.

Yeah, he had it bad.

He joined her, taking an edge of the blanket and spreading it in front of the fire. He couldn't wait to see the warm glow worship every inch of her skin. Because he planned to kneel at that particular altar himself for most of the night.

When he moved toward her, she shook her head, making him frown. Then he realized why, when she pulled the turtleneck over her head, revealing a peach bra that was so thin he could see the buds of her nipples pressed tight against the satiny fabric. Jack's mouth watered.

Her hands went to her back.

"Don't take it off," he murmured.

She bit her lip but did as he asked, leaving the garment in place. Her fingers toyed with the button on her jeans, glancing at him in question.

"Definitely."

His body hardened, a thumping going through his head as she undid her pants and slowly pushed them down her hips.

Her panties matched her bra, just like they had the last time they'd been together, but there were no ties on the sides this time. That was okay. There were plenty of ways to get those off her. Or not. Depending on how he felt when the time actually came.

Right now, his brain was tapping out *Hurry* in

some kind of weird Morse code. He ignored it. No hurrying. Not tonight.

She stepped out of the jeans and kicked them to the side, before getting on her knees on the blanket. Crooking a finger at him, she motioned him closer. When he went to kneel in front of her, she gripped the knees of his jeans and hauled him closer, keeping him on his feet.

Did she know how close she was? How suggestive her position was?

"Your turn," she said. With that, she used both hands to open his button and then unzip his fly.

His turn to what? Get undressed?

He had his answer soon enough when she tugged his pants and briefs down to his knees, freeing him. He gave an internal curse. He was right. He was in line with a very warm and wet area, and his body was sending out all kinds of messages. But he wasn't going that route. Not without a clear sign from her.

Her hands went around him, and she glanced up at him. "Like I said, it's your turn. Come here."

It suddenly dawned on him. She was referring

to their last encounter when he'd put her up on that bar and had his way with her.

She was about to turn the tables.

Sinking his fingers in her hair, he slowly closed his fist around the silky strands and edged her closer. That gorgeous mouth opened right on cue. So very, very close.

Hell.

"Do it." His muttered words were rough, surprising even him.

Mira closed the gap, the heat of her mouth engulfing him in a slow glide that had him shuddering with need. Hot flames licked at his body as her hands left his erection and went to the backs of his thighs, curling around them, hauling him even closer.

His vision went white, all sensation pooling at the points of contact between them, her tongue sliding over his length in a single smooth stroke that made him wonder if he was going to lose it right here. Right now.

No. That's not what he wanted.

When he went to step away, though, she followed him, forcing him to reach back and grip her wrists, tugging them away so he could put some space between them. The popping sound of lost suction created an agonizing mixture of triumph and despair inside him that he was in no hurry to erase. But he was in a hurry for something else.

Still holding her wrists, he hauled her to her feet, insides steaming with heat when she gazed up at him and licked her lips. "Not fair," she murmured. "I wasn't done yet."

"You were done all right." In another few seconds he would have been as well. He moved her wrists behind her back and held them there with one hand, while he palmed the back of her head with the other, holding her still so he could capture her mouth. His tongue plunged inside, a demonstration of what he had in store for her, and he used his hold on her wrists to press her abdomen against him, trapping himself between their bodies. It wasn't nearly enough, but he had to somehow slow this train wreck down.

He let go of her hands, sliding up to find the clasp on her bra and releasing it. Then he stepped back yet again, taking the straps with him, allowing the silky garment to drop onto the blanket. Then he tugged his shirt over his head and finished losing the rest of his clothes.

Allowing his gaze to slide over her, he reveled in the toned limbs that came with skiing and working in the snow and ice, and the pale creamy skin that went so perfectly with a chilly climate. No tanning beds for this ice princess.

Only she wasn't made of ice. She was hot and smooth and made him ache like no one ever had before. He held out his arms, and she came into them willingly, her nipples pressing against him, her silk panties welcoming his hands as he slid beneath the back of them and cupped her bottom. Hell, he wanted to be inside her. Wanted to thrust and grunt all the way to completion, but part of his pleasure was watching her come apart beneath his hands. So he set about making that happen, allowing his lips and teeth to trail from her face to her neck and finally to the tips of her breasts until her low moan washed over him.

Yes.

This was what he wanted more than anything: to be what brought her to life and led her down that sensual path until she could no longer resist its pull.

His tongue scrubbed over her nipple, letting the sounds she made guide how long he visited, how much pressure he used. And the woman could take a lot, fingers thrust into his hair pressing him closer and urging him to be just a little rougher.

Jack's body let him know in no uncertain terms that it wanted in on the action, the ache ramping up to almost painful proportions. When she moaned again, his flesh jerked in a silent plea.

Soon.

Still beneath her panties, his hand slid from her butt around to the front and edged deeper, his fingers finding a familiar sweet heat…and damp readiness. He stroked over her, moving to kiss her mouth as those delectable little sounds increased in frequency.

Making his decision, he pulled free, wrapped one arm around her thighs and slid the other beneath her shoulders. He swept her off her feet and onto the blanket, following her down.

He kissed her hard and wet and long, feeling her arch against him.

Off came the panties. One knee went between her legs.

Anticipation roared through him as he slid a finger deep inside her, thumb going to that sensitive nub of flesh and stroking over it in gentle flicks that had him quivering with need.

"Jack." Her back arched again.

That was all the encouragement it took for him to slide his body into the gap between her thighs and surge forward. He found her, just as he'd expected. Hot and tight and slick with her own need.

He swallowed, knowing he'd waited too long. His body was tightly wound, full, ready to burst open at the slightest move.

"Hold on, sweetheart, it's going to be a bumpy ride."

Struggling to keep himself in check, he thrust again and again, concentrating on hitting that one vital spot at the top of her legs. Legs that wrapped around him, pulling him deeper and harder as she lifted her hips and plastered herself against him the second they made contact again. She ground and gasped and wiggled, eyes closing tight as that final wave of sensation swept toward them. It crashed over her first, the sudden tightening of her flesh around his unleashing a torrent inside him. He rode the crest a second or two longer before finally succumbing and tumbling headlong into the surf, allowing it to carry him all the way back to shore.

He lay there for several seconds, not sure if he was stunned into immobility or if he'd died and rocketed straight into heaven. All he knew was that there was no place he'd rather be than right here in this woman's arms.

And that fact terrified him. Paralyzed him.

Because one act had just cost him everything.

In rushing to the finish line, Jack had lost much more than the fight with his body. He'd also lost the battle with his heart.

Jack had been quiet the whole ride back to the lodge the next day. They'd gone to bed the previous night, where he'd held her, looping his arm around her as they'd slept. But he hadn't tried to make love to her again, unlike the previous time they'd been together.

She wasn't sure if she'd done something wrong or if it was just him.

Part of her was afraid she'd appeared too desperate and needy, grabbing at him and giving herself that last burst of pleasure. But it had been too late to stop by that point. And he'd seemed to like it at the time, groaning encouragement into her ear and increasing his pace.

But afterwards he'd seemed strange, rolling off her and staring at the ceiling for several long seconds. He'd recovered and pulled her to her feet, giving her a quick kiss on the mouth before offering to let her use the shower first.

First. Not together.

They'd eaten a canned dinner of stuff they'd found in the pantry, but the mood had been somber as they'd sat on the couch later, facing the fire, Jack's arm around her.

What had he been thinking?

If she'd said something, he'd responded, but emotionally he'd seemed to have withdrawn.

Today she'd treated a couple of patients, giving one teenager a lecture on helmet usage when he'd appeared with a lump on his forehead after falling on the slopes, and hugging a child who'd had a boo-boo on her finger—courtesy of a sharp pinch from a door. Neither were serious injuries.

Unlike the weird volley of emotions that soared through her chest one second and fell into the pit of her stomach the next, only to bounce up and start the cycle all over. It was exhausting.

She slumped in a chair in the dining room, picking at her salad. Ellory was off hiking by herself for the day. She'd left a note at the front desk that she'd check in with Mira later and that she hoped her outing with Number Five had been productive—and hot. She had a "feeling" about this one.

So did Mira. And it wasn't a good feeling.

In fact, it was as ominous as the weather forecast for the coming week. There was the threat of the first big storm of the season. Moisture was gathering to the southwest and there was a high-pressure system in the northeast that was preparing to send a frigid blast of air their way. When those two forces combined, things could get dicey over the next five days. At just over twelve thousand feet elevation, Silver Pass was almost sure to get a large portion of that snowfall, if it arrived. Already the resort was busy preparing behind the scenes while trying not to worry any of their guests. The storm could very well peter out. She'd met with her dad this morning for breakfast, but he'd been distracted about the preparations.

If only she could be just as diligent to prepare for any eventuality with Jack. But without even a vague forecast to go by, there was nothing she could do. Oh, she could tell him she was reneging on their deal, that she didn't want to see him any more for the duration of his stay. But what if she was overreacting?

A man's shoes came into view beside her table. Her heart leap-frogged over itself as she jerked her head up, only to land with a clunk when she realized it was Robert. Great, just what she needed.

"Mind if I join you?" he asked.

She motioned to the chair across from hers. "Help yourself."

He set his coffee on the table and then dropped into the seat. "We never did get a chance to talk."

"About what?" Lord, she really didn't want to rehash their whole breakup.

"Your dad came out to see me a few hours ago," he said. "Did you tell him about us?"

"Yes. Why? Did he say something?"

He shook his head, lips pursing. "No. He really just talked about how long to keep the slopes open, if this storm hits."

Leaning back, he ran a hand through wavy blond locks that had always reminded her of a Norse god. She could see why women were attracted to him. But he no longer did anything for her.

"Okay, I'm not sure I understand, then. Are you worried?"

"I just want to know exactly what you told him. Do I need to look for another job?"

Ah, so that's what he was worried about. With his snarky comments of late, maybe she should let him sweat for a while. But since she was finding out first hand how it felt to be kept in the dark about someone's intentions, she didn't wish that on anyone. Not even Robert.

"Whether or not you look for another job is up to you. If he asks for specifics, I just plan on telling him the truth, that we both realized it wasn't going to work and decided to break our engagement." She shrugged. "So as long as you keep doing your job, you should have nothing to worry about."

"Thank you." In a move that was not in character for the self-assured cocky man she knew, he covered her hand with his and gave it a squeeze before tucking a lock of hair behind her ear. "I know it doesn't mean anything, but I want you to know I'm sorry for how things went down. I should have had the courage to tell you up front that I wasn't ready to settle down."

You mean before you made out with that bimbo and several others? Yeah, you could have saved us both a whole lot of grief—and saved me from a clunker of a resolution.

One she no longer wanted to keep.

She didn't say any of that, though. "What's

done is done. I recommend honesty the next time you get involved with someone."

His lips gave a rueful twist. "Understood." He hesitated. "If later on down the line—"

"If you're going to say what I think you are, then no. You're right. It wouldn't have worked."

"Is it because of that guy you've been hanging around?"

Mira swallowed, trying to divert her thoughts to something else. It didn't work. Jack's face popped into her mind—the way his eyes had darkened as he'd settled over her last night.

Lord. Robert was right. It was because of Jack. That's why she was so sure it could never work with him, even if she found out he hadn't been cheating.

She was in love with Number Five. Someone she knew beyond the shadow of a doubt would never cheat on the person he loved. He'd shown that in how he talked about his wife…the guilt he carried about how she died.

Mira just…knew.

Maybe she really could tell the good guys from the bad.

And she loved him—for that reason and so many more.

The knowledge was both exhilarating and devastating. He'd made it clear he wasn't looking for anything serious.

But with you, I find myself wanting a next time. And a next.

Jack's words from last night whispered through her mind, then rewound and played back all over again.

It certainly wasn't something she was going to admit to Robert, though.

"I'm not involved with anyone. Nor am I planning to be. I'm just not interested in giving us another chance."

He gazed at her for a second before giving a slow nod. "Okay. Let me know if you change your mind. I'll be around."

With that, he picked up his insulated drink carrier and walked away.

Right past Number Five, who was standing not three feet away, his own coffee cup in hand. His eyes were on them.

Oh, God. How much of their conversation had he just heard?

Enough, evidently, since he veered away and chose a table twenty feet away.

Oh, no, he didn't. If he wanted nothing to do with her, he was going to have to tell her flat out.

Leaving the remainder of her salad uneaten, she got up and went over to his table and pulled out a chair. Unlike Robert, though, she didn't ask if she could sit. She just did.

"Hi," she said. For all her bravado, her heart was slipping around in her chest like a skier who'd just realized the run he was on was way above his skill level.

Jack's fingers tightened on his mug. "Hey. Hope I didn't run him off."

"You didn't." She licked her lips. "How are you?"

"That's the question of the year, isn't it?"

"I'm sorry?"

He blew out a rough breath. "Nothing."

After several beats went by, she decided to test the waters. "About yesterday—"

"Yeah, I was just coming to talk to you about

that." Another pause. "You love it here, Mira, don't you?"

"Silver Pass? Yes, of course I do. I grew up here. Why?"

"No reason. Just curious."

That was a strange thing to be curious about. Besides, what did it have to do with yesterday?

Before she could turn back to that particular subject, Jack started in again.

"I don't know if you've seen the weather forecast, but I'm due back in Texas in a little over a week, just after that storm is supposed to hit. I don't want to take the chance on my flight being canceled if it's worse than predicted, so…"

He was leaving. Not in a week. But soon. Maybe even today.

"When are you going?"

"They're trying to book me on any flight they can get, so I figured I wouldn't have time to track you down and say goodbye. The reception desk told me you were in here, so I thought…" his jaw tightened "…now was as good a time as any."

As good a time as any? As if she were no more important than any other business acquaintance.

She guessed that put her in her place. If he wanted to tell her exactly where she stood, he couldn't have chosen a better way to let her down easy.

Only it wasn't easy. But she wasn't going to drop to her knees and beg him not to go. He had a job back in Texas. She'd known that from the very beginning.

That was one thing living at a ski resort taught you, that people were not permanent fixtures. They came and they went. An endless cycle that could bring heartache, if you let it. Isn't that what she'd been trying to teach herself with her resolution? That she needed to let them wander through while keeping her heart away from those high-traffic areas?

God. And look how successful she'd been at that.

"Well, it's been fun. Thank you." She swallowed. "Have a good flight."

When she stood to go, he grabbed her wrist, fingers tight against her skin. "It was more than fun, and you know it. I just can't do...this."

This. *This?* What the hell "this" was he talking about?

She had no idea. But whatever it was, he didn't want it. Didn't want her.

Her chin went up. "I don't remember anyone asking you to."

There. Way to lob it right back at him, Mira.

Instead of pride, though, all she felt was sadness…and that same weird desperation she'd felt in his arms last night.

Number Five was leaving, and she hadn't even had to tell him to go.

She could try to convince him not to. Tell him how she felt. But did she really want to grasp at someone who…what was it that Robert had said? Oh, yes, who just "wasn't ready to settle down"—with her or with anyone.

Jack released her and the fingers of her other hand rubbed at the spot, trying to erase the memory of his touch. It didn't work, though. He'd branded himself on her. Not last night. Not that time in his hotel room. But that very first time their hands had gripped each other's in the snow.

And now she had to find a way—like he had—to uncurl her fingers and let him go.

CHAPTER TWELVE

"WHAT DO YOU mean, he's leaving early?"

Ellory's face was a study in disbelief as she stood in Mira's room, hands on her hips.

"There's talk of a winter storm blowing in, and he's afraid of getting stranded."

"Oh, he's afraid all right, but not of getting stranded. What happened?"

Mira went through the whole story, about how they'd gone to the lodge, how everything had seemed to be going really well, about how he'd talked about his wife's death.

"He told you about that?"

Mira nodded. "Why?"

"That's not something you tell someone you have no intention of ever seeing again. Why would he bother, unless he felt it was something you needed to know?"

Mira dropped onto the foot of her bed and

grabbed her Cheshire cat. "He started acting funny right after we…" she rolled her hand around in the air "…you know."

"After you boinked like bunnies in front of the fire?"

"Elle!"

Her friend grinned and then sprawled next to her, poking the stuffed cat in its furry little belly. "You were supposed to teach her a thing or two about loosening up."

Oh, she'd been plenty loose. That was her problem. If she'd held on to her emotions just a little bit tighter, she could have avoided this whole mess.

That wasn't true, and she knew it.

"Okay," Ellory said. "Let's go down the list of things we know. One, his wife died in a plane crash. Two, he asked that you two see each other exclusively while he was here at the resort. Have I got it right so far?"

"Yes, but—"

"I'm thinking here." She put a finger to her lips and tapped. "Three, after he tells you about his wife, you get down to business and then he seems weird afterwards."

Mira nodded. "I thought I was being too forward."

"Get real, ninny. Men love that stuff. So what happened after that?"

Impatience flared to life. She'd wanted hugs and a sympathetic shoulder, not to write a dissertation on what had gone wrong. "What does it matter?"

"It matters."

Mira's brows went up. "Okay. Four. He asks me if I like it here in Silver Pass. Five. He says there's a storm coming…says he's leaving early." Her voice sped up as another wave of hurt rolled through her. "I reply that it's been fun, bye. He grabs me and says it was more than that, and that I know it, but he just can't do…" she drew quotes in the air "…*this*."

"This."

"Yeah, one minute he's asking me about Silver… Oh, my God." Wrapping her arms around her stomach, she let Chessie slide to the floor. "He can't ask me to leave. That's what it is."

"What?"

"Silver Pass. His wife died on the flight to Texas. She'd left her job to be with him."

Ellory picked up the cat and tossed it onto the pillows behind them. "He's afraid you'll die?"

"I don't think so. Or at least I hope he's not irrational enough to think it could happen twice. I think his guilt won't let him ask me to choose between him and the resort. He asked me if I loved Silver Pass. Right out of the blue, after he saw me talking to Robert. It didn't go along with anything we were talking about. I thought it was strange at the time, since he said he wanted to talk about what had happened at the cabin."

"I think you're right, Mirri." Her brows went up. "So what's stopping you?"

"From what? He's probably already left."

"So? It's not like you can't find Texas. It's freaking huge. Right there on every map."

Mira closed her eyes. Her friend was right. What was stopping her?

Fear.

Fear of rejection. Fear of what she'd find when she saw him. Fear…that he didn't love her.

And?

What more did she have to lose? She'd let him walk away—so he was gone already as far as that went. If she confronted him, and he said he didn't want to be with her, she hadn't lost anything more. Just a small chunk of her pride.

But she deserved to know how he felt once and for all.

"You're right. It's on the map." She reached over and grabbed her friend and squeezed her hard. "Thank you, Elle. Wish me luck."

"I already did that when you made your resolution." She laughed. "I sent out a little note to the universe, asking them to let *me* win our little bet. Which meant that Number Five—well, like Obi Wan Kenobi, he was my only hope."

Jack slid his sunglasses higher on his nose as he waited in line at the airport. It had taken more than one attempt to finally walk out of the door of the resort this morning, two weeks to the day from when he'd first set foot on that ski slope and seen Mira standing over him.

He'd left two things behind. One thing meant nothing. And one meant everything.

The nothing: his pills, which he'd flushed down the toilet the day after his and Mira's little trip to the cabin. He wouldn't be needing them any more. It was time to face his fears and his dreams.

The everything: Mira. He still couldn't believe he'd found the strength to walk away.

But he wasn't going to ask her to leave. The words had been on the tip of his tongue, but he'd bitten them back. The storm was just an excuse, but she didn't need to know that. It had come just in the nick of time, saving him from making the same mistake with another woman that he'd made with his wife.

If she wanted to stay in Silver Pass, he wasn't going to be the one who urged her to leave.

And what if Mira had asked him to stay, rather than the other way around? Would he have?

His mind toyed with that idea for a few minutes. Yeah. He probably would have. But he'd never given her the opportunity to do anything except say goodbye. He'd cut her off before she could even have her say.

And what if she'd wanted more? More of their days together? More of making love? More…of everything?

Hadn't she earned the right to be heard?

Yes. He sucked down a breath. And maybe he should do something about that.

Whether it had been a mistake to ask his wife to move for the sake of his job was a moot point. What was done was done—he couldn't go back and change it, no matter how much he might wish to.

But he could change how he went on from here. What if—instead of asking Mira to leave—he asked her if he could stay in Silver Pass? With her?

It would mean giving up his job with the Hawks, but he could practice medicine anywhere. It didn't even have to be with a sports team. In fact, he could imagine his services might be in high demand in any of the hospitals around a ski resort.

His heart hadn't been in his job for a while. The coach knew it, which was why he'd sent him on this vacation in the first place. To clear his head. To help him make a choice.

It had worked. What he wanted out of life had never been clearer to him than it was right now.

Decision made, he tore the plane ticket in half and then in half again, continuing the process until the stack was too thick to rip any further. Then he stuffed all the pieces inside his coat pocket and got out of line, his pace quickening as he caught sight of the exit across the concourse.

"Jack!" A familiar voice came from somewhere behind him.

The sound stopped him in his tracks.

In slow motion, he turned. But he didn't see anything other than folks hurrying to the security check-in area. It must have been his imagination. Then a hand waved from the line he'd just vacated.

Mira. What was she doing here?

He stood there for a second, before making his way back to the line. She met him halfway.

"What's going on?" he asked, taking in the hair she'd tugged back in a ponytail, her lightweight jacket. Much too light for the mountains.

She held out a slip of paper. "I have a plane ticket to Texas. On your flight, in fact. If you want me."

He blinked, staring at her hand, her words not registering for a second or two.

She'd chosen to come with him. Of her own volition. Just like he'd chosen to stay here in Silver Pass.

Jack laughed—the first really free chuckle he'd allowed himself in almost four years.

"What's so funny?" she demanded.

He pulled the torn pieces of his ticket from his pocket. "This."

"I don't understand."

"You just bought a ticket. And I just shredded one."

Shock flashed through her eyes. "You did? Why?"

"Because I don't want to leave. Not yet."

"But the storm… Your job—"

"Can all wait," he said. "I needed to come back and find you." He blew out a breath, not sure where to start. "When I went to the restaurant two days ago I had everything planned out in my head. What I was going to say. What I was going to do. How hard I was going to kiss you."

"You were?"

He nodded. Oh, how he'd screwed up his courage, only to have it desert him at the last minute. "And then I saw you there with Robert. Heard him try to win you back and realized you could have so much more if you found someone from Silver Pass. If you spent your life loving a man who shared your life, your passions…your location."

"But—"

"Wait." He set his bag down and slung an arm around her shoulders, his heart growing lighter by the second. This was what he should have done at the restaurant. Especially after seeing her beautiful face standing in the line of passengers behind him. "As I was in that line, I started thinking. Why couldn't *I* be that man?"

"What?"

"I love you, Mira. I know nothing about the mountains, and I don't know how to ski or how to ride a snowboard or even a snowmobile. But I swear I'll be true and that I'll spend the rest of life learning about all those things. If you'll have me."

Mira stared up at him for a minute and then turned toward him, burying her face in his chest, her shoulders shaking.

What the hell?

She'd bought a ticket. Surely she couldn't be that blind that she hadn't read the signs…figured out how he felt. But then again, he wasn't sure about her feelings either, just assumed that buying a ticket to Texas meant she cared about him. "What's wrong?"

She leaned back, her eyes streaming, swiping away the tears with her palm. Her body still shook. It was then he realized she wasn't crying. She was laughing.

"Wh-what's wrong?" she asked between gasps. "I was going to say the exact same thing. I even ordered a surfboard to be sent to the team's address—guess they'll be surprised when that package is delivered, huh?"

"You ordered a surfboard?"

She sucked down a deep breath. "I did. I love you too. And I *want* to be where you are, Jack.

You're not forcing me to leave. I *want* to." Her teeth came down on her lip. "Although I have a confession to make."

His chest tightened. "What's that?"

"I'm deathly afraid of sharks. Think you can still teach me how to surf?"

He smiled and planted a hard kiss on her mouth, forcing himself not to linger more than a minute or two. "I think that's something we should discuss in detail. Back at the lodge. Because I suddenly have a very urgent need."

"Anything I can help with?"

He kissed her again. "Actually, you're the only one who can."

Three hours later they were snuggled together under the covers in her room, perspiration still drying on her skin. Jack lay behind her, his body pressed tight to hers, thumb brushing back and forth over her bare hip. A shiver went through her.

God, she loved this man. No matter where the future took them, she wanted to be right in the middle of it.

"Does this mean you're not moving on to guy number six any time soon?" The low gravelly tones slid across her temple, carrying more than a hint of possessiveness.

"Mmm. I'll think about it."

The hand caressing her hip dropped a quick slap to her butt.

"Oww. Okay. No more men." She blinked as the stinging in her backside morphed into a wave of heat that washed over her. "Although your reaction to that *was* kind of hot."

Something came to life against the swell of her bottom.

"Woman, you are going to be the death of me."

She rolled onto her other side. "What about the storm? Are you sure you don't need to go back? I'll go with you." She touched his face. "Because I want to. Not because I have to. My dad is getting married in a few months, and I've already talked to him about finding a replacement for me."

"I still have a few things to work out in my head, and you need to know what you're getting into. I've struggled over the last four years."

"It's okay. We have plenty of time to figure things out. It doesn't even matter where we end up."

He drew her closer. "For now, I just want to ride out the storm here at the lodge. With you."

"Emphasis on the riding part, I hope."

"Mira!" He gave a half-strangled laugh that lit her up inside.

She snuggled back against him. "I guess this means I owe Ellory a hundred bucks. She bet I wouldn't make it past man number five without falling for him."

Jack turned her over and took her mouth in a long kiss that had her clinging to him, breathless for more. "A hundred bucks, huh? Not sure I'm worth that kind of money."

She reached beneath the covers and found him, already hard and ready.

"Well, then," she said. "I guess you'd better start earning your keep."

She stroked him once and then again, relishing the low groan of pleasure he gave at her touch.

"Mmm…I think I could get used to this." He rolled her beneath him and parted her legs.

"How long do you think it'll take me to pay off that debt?"

She arched into him, her own need beginning to rise out of control. "How does forever sound?"

* * * * *

MILLS & BOON®
Large Print Medical

August

A DATE WITH HER VALENTINE DOC	Melanie Milburne
IT HAPPENED IN PARIS...	Robin Gianna
THE SHEIKH DOCTOR'S BRIDE	Meredith Webber
TEMPTATION IN PARADISE	Joanna Neil
A BABY TO HEAL THEIR HEARTS	Kate Hardy
THE SURGEON'S BABY SECRET	Amber McKenzie

September

BABY TWINS TO BIND THEM	Carol Marinelli
THE FIREFIGHTER TO HEAL HER HEART	Annie O'Neil
TORTURED BY HER TOUCH	Dianne Drake
IT HAPPENED IN VEGAS	Amy Ruttan
THE FAMILY SHE NEEDS	Sue MacKay
A FATHER FOR POPPY	Abigail Gordon

October

JUST ONE NIGHT?	Carol Marinelli
MEANT-TO-BE FAMILY	Marion Lennox
THE SOLDIER SHE COULD NEVER FORGET	Tina Beckett
THE DOCTOR'S REDEMPTION	Susan Carlisle
WANTED: PARENTS FOR A BABY!	Laura Iding
HIS PERFECT BRIDE?	Louisa Heaton

MILLS & BOON®
Large Print Medical

November

ALWAYS THE MIDWIFE	Alison Roberts
MIDWIFE'S BABY BUMP	Susanne Hampton
A KISS TO MELT HER HEART	Emily Forbes
TEMPTED BY HER ITALIAN SURGEON	Louisa George
DARING TO DATE HER EX	Annie Claydon
THE ONE MAN TO HEAL HER	Meredith Webber

December

MIDWIFE...TO MUM!	Sue MacKay
HIS BEST FRIEND'S BABY	Susan Carlisle
ITALIAN SURGEON TO THE STARS	Melanie Milburne
HER GREEK DOCTOR'S PROPOSAL	Robin Gianna
NEW YORK DOC TO BLUSHING BRIDE	Janice Lynn
STILL MARRIED TO HER EX!	Lucy Clark

January

UNLOCKING HER SURGEON'S HEART	Fiona Lowe
HER PLAYBOY'S SECRET	Tina Beckett
THE DOCTOR SHE LEFT BEHIND	Scarlet Wilson
TAMING HER NAVY DOC	Amy Ruttan
A PROMISE...TO A PROPOSAL?	Kate Hardy
HER FAMILY FOR KEEPS	Molly Evans

0715 LP 2P P2 Medic